NO ONE TO TRUST

RED STONE SECURITY SERIES

Katie Reus

For my mom.

Praise for the novels of Katie Reus

Secrets are what keep a family strong. United. Elizabeth Martinez could still hear her father's words echoing in the recesses of her memories. Over a decade had passed and not a day went by that she didn't wish she could rewrite history. Some secrets had a way of eating a person alive. From the inside out, one giant bite at a time. Gnawing until she couldn't stand it. If her father hadn't forced them all to keep the family's dirty little secret, maybe she'd be at home enjoying a nice glass of wine and a bubble bath. She wouldn't be picking up her brother from a drug dealer's house on a chilly Tuesday evening.

Lizzy put her BMW into park and slid from the vehicle. This particular mansion in Keystone Island was the last place in the world she wanted to be. Unfortunately her brother had called begging for help. Again.

Everyone else in the family had turned their back on Benny but she simply couldn't say no when he needed her. Not when he'd always been there for her.

While she wasn't sure what Benny was doing at the recently deceased Alberto Salas's home, she knew it couldn't be good. Salas had been infamous for running drugs up and down the entire East Coast. She'd heard his son, Orlando, had taken over his operation. She'd briefly interacted with Orlando at a few charity functions around Miami and he'd always been perfectly polite, but the man gave her the creeps. There were some things an Armani suit simply couldn't hide.

Self-consciously, Lizzy tugged at her dress as if she could somehow make it grow a couple inches longer. The bright turquoise halter-style dress and black cardigan sweater she wore were completely respectable, but as she walked down the stone driveway toward the front door, she could feel several sets of eyes on her. Considering Orlando Salas was rumored to be in the same business his father had been, she guessed that even though she couldn't see them, he had plenty of scary looking security guys milling around. They were nothing more than thugs in suits and ties. She worked for one of the best security firms in the nation and the guys she worked with—they sure weren't thugs. No, they were highly trained, mostly ex-military, and didn't deal with scum like Salas. They protected uber wealthy clients and government dignitaries and everyone they worked for got a detailed military level background check—courtesy of her computer skills—and if it appeared they were into anything like drugs, Red Stone Security didn't take them on. With how much money their company made, they could afford to be picky.

Before she could knock on the bright red door, it swung open and a man carrying an assault rifle looked her up and down.

A cold chill slithered through her, mainly because of the look on his face, rather than the gun. She'd known the guards here would be armed, but *yuck*, this guy made her feel like she was naked. Clutching her purse tighter against her side—as if that could somehow save her—she started to tell him why she was there, but he beat her to it.

With a lecherous grin on his face, he stepped back and allowed her to enter. "Your brother's out back." He pointed down the tile hallway. "Just follow until you reach the French doors."

Fighting back the growing panic humming through her, she nodded and did just as he said. Yeah, maybe she should have called her boss and told him what she was doing but she didn't want to drag anyone she knew into Benny's problems. Then everyone would know how messed up her family really was. It was too embarrassing. She'd take care of it just like she always had. *Chin up*, she ordered herself.

As she neared the doors she could see her brother stretched out on an Adirondack chair. She yanked the door open and hurried to his still form. "Benny!"

When he didn't stir, an icy fist clasped around her heart. He looked like a corpse. His normally bronze face was a grayish color. She touched his wrist and a sharp burst of relief popped inside her. At least his pulse was strong. But his face...tears blurred her vision for a moment. A garish purple bruise covered his left cheek and one of his eyes was swollen almost all the way shut. A light trail of blood had trickled from his nostril and dried on his upper lip. Had they broke his nose? Her throat tightened with raw grief. He'd sounded bad on the phone but she hadn't expected *this*. She wanted to touch him, comfort him somehow, but was afraid she'd only hurt him more.

Her hand hovered over his pale face for a moment before she settled on brushing a lock of his dark hair away from his forehead. "What have you gotten yourself into," she whispered.

"He's going to be out for a little while." She swiveled around at a familiar male voice and let her hand drop.

Monster. The word echoed inside her but she bit it back. "Mr. Salas." She tried to keep the disdain out of her voice as she faced the man who'd likely beaten her brother. Or at least watched while one of his men had. Somehow she managed to blink back the tears threatening to spill over.

"Please call me Orlando. You're a very good sister to pick your brother up so quickly." Standing about ten feet away from her, he leaned against the mini-bar with a glass tumbler in hand.

She narrowed her gaze. Anger battled with the fear blossoming inside her but she was still level-headed enough not to cower in front of him. A man like this probably craved the fear of others. "Did you do this to him?"

His shoulders lifted in a slight shrug. "Not personally. Benito owes me quite a bit of money and I intend to collect."

"How much?"

"A hundred thousand."

Lizzy swallowed but tried to school her shock. Benny had had problems with drugs in the past but he'd been clean for a while. Unfortunately, he'd found a new drug of choice. Gambling. If she had to guess, he owed Orlando the money because of bad bets. Or maybe he was back into drugs. She just didn't know. And she hated what her brother did to himself. He had such a good heart but he couldn't seem to keep it together.

Her parents had the money. *She* definitely didn't. And it was unlikely her parents would fork over that kind of cash for the black sheep of the family. Unless she could convince them it was for her. Despite the terror splintering through her, she stood her ground. "So you tried to *beat* the money out of him?"

His dark gaze seemed to penetrate right through to her innermost thoughts. "He's lucky he's not dead. Out of respect for your family, I'm giving him one week to pay me back."

"And if he doesn't?" She hated that the question came out shaky, but she couldn't help it. She was scared, even if she tried to hide it.

"I sincerely hope he has a life insurance policy." He placed his glass on the bar and covered the short distance between them in seconds. Before she could react, he'd pressed her against one of the columns lining the outer edges of the lanai. His breath was hot on her cheek and his expensive cologne nearly smothered her as fear clawed at her insides. "I might be willing to bargain, however, Ms. Martinez. You are a beautiful woman. Six months as mine, and I'll let your brother off." His hips jerked forward and she pushed back the bile in her throat when she felt his erection against her hip.

Instinct overtook her fear as she shoved at his chest. "You're disgusting."

He was immovable. Grabbing her wrist, he pinned it above her head. When she swung out at him with her other hand, he snapped it up with the same precision. She tried to tug against him, but the man's grip was like an iron shackle. Cold sweat blossomed across her forehead and spread the length of her body. She hadn't told anyone where she was going, and Orlando Salas was total scum. If he raped her, he wouldn't let her live to tell anyone. No, he'd likely dump her in the ocean. She racked her brain, trying to think of a way out of her situation when a loud shout and glass breaking inside caused him to let her go. But not before he backhanded her across the face and growled, "Stay here."

The abrupt action surprised her more than it hurt. A dull throb spread across her cheek, but it was nothing compared to what would happen to her if she didn't get out of there. As he started to reach for a gun tucked in the back of his pants, the double doors flew open and the last person she expected to see stormed through, with a SIG in hand.

And it was pointed directly at Orlando.

"Are you okay, Elizabeth?" Porter Caldwell, her unlikely savior, asked in his typical clipped tone.

"I'm fine." At the moment, all that mattered was getting out of there alive. She wasn't exactly sure what Porter was doing there or even how he'd gotten past Orlando's guards. She wasn't going to balk at a chance to escape, even if her rescuer was her sort-of-ex/almost-lover. Even though they'd dated for a month and gotten pretty physical, they'd never actually had sex so she didn't think that qualified him as an old lover.

"Do you know who I am?" Orlando spat, but Lizzy noticed he didn't continue reaching for his gun. He wasn't that stupid.

Porter's pale blue gaze narrowed with deadly precision. "More importantly, do you know who *I* am?"

Without waiting for a response, he strode toward Orlando and slammed the gun across his head with a vicious blow.

With a short-lived cry of surprise, Orlando crumpled onto the mosaic tile. Lizzy had expected more of a response from the man but maybe without his security to back him up he wasn't so tough after all.

Porter grabbed Lizzy's wrist and started tugging her toward the open doors. "We have maybe sixty seconds to get out of here before the rest of his guards realize what's going on. I don't know what the hell you're doing here, but—"

She yanked hard against his grasp. "My brother!"

He paused to stare at her, his gaze unreadable. "What?"

She nodded at Benny. "We need to get him out of here too."

His head cocked slightly to the side as if seeing the crumpled heap that was her brother for the first time. Mr. Tall, dark and annoyed muttered something under his breath before tucking his gun away. Then he lifted her brother onto his shoulder as if he weighed nothing. Benny was almost six feet tall but Porter was taller and much broader. And all muscle. "Follow me," he grunted.

Clutching her purse to her side, she hurried after Porter. "What are you doing here?" she whispered.

"Saving your pretty little butt. Ask your questions later. We need to get the hell out of here." His shoes were silent against the tile while her heels clacked noisily. If she didn't think it would slow her down she'd take them off and run in her bare feet. When they reached the open foyer, she spotted two guards unconscious and face down on the tile. Broken shards of what had once been a vase littered around one of the men.

Fear skittered along her exposed skin. "I don't understand—"

"Your car. Now," he barked as he jerked the front door open. He didn't even glance behind him as he strode outside.

Not bothering to pull the front door shut behind her, she started to slide into the passenger side of her car while Porter dumped Benny in the back. Before she'd even shut her door, Porter kicked the car into drive and sped off.

"What...what are you doing here?" She hated that her voice shook but she couldn't control it. She was grateful he'd shown up but she hated that he'd seen her and her brother in this kind of situation. Keeping her family life private was too important. And Porter had already made it clear what he thought of her brother. She didn't like giving him more ammunition against Benny.

"Don't you know what kind of man Orlando Salas is?" he ground out. It wasn't so much a question as a statement of disgust.

As he sped down the stone driveway, she glanced behind them to see two men running out the front door, guns in hand. At least they didn't open fire on them. Thankfully the iron gate was still open as Porter tore through the opening. "How'd you get past his security? And where's your car? And why are you even here?"

"I'm going to pretend you didn't ask that first question," he muttered and chose to ignore her other two questions completely.

She bit back a retort and tried to take a few steadying breaths. Porter might drive her crazy with his bossy attitude, but Lizzy worked for Red Stone Security, which was owned by his father. And his brother Harrison was her boss. Not that she had any fear Harrison would fire her if she got into it with Porter, but still, she liked to pick her battles wisely. As the peacemaker of her family she was used to stopping fights, not starting them.

She glanced over her shoulder again and was relieved to see that no one was following them. Turning to Porter, she said, "Explain how you knew I was at Orlando Salas's house." She figured she probably should have asked nicely, not demanded an answer, but right now she felt as if her insides were actually shaking.

He shot her a sharp glance that put her on edge, but at the same time made something annoyingly feminine inside her flare to life. Without even trying the man exuded a raw sexuality that made her abdomen clench with need each time she saw him. Or thought about him. Lately that was too often.

"I put a GPS tracker in your car a couple weeks ago," he said quietly.

It took a moment for his words to register. She shook her head, sure she'd misheard. "*What?*"

He shrugged and made another left turn. "It was the only way I knew to keep you safe."

"Safe? What... Do you realize how crazy this sounds? You put a *tracker* in my car!" The tiny voice in the back of her head told her to shut up and be grateful he had considering what had just happened.

His sharp features never changed as he pulled up behind an SUV parked by the curb. He fished out a set of keys and handed them to her. "I want you to drive my vehicle and I'll follow you back to your place."

She sputtered and stared at his outstretched hand.

"Lizzy, please. I'll answer all your questions once we get out of here."

His use of her nickname took her off guard. He rarely called her Lizzy. The first time had been right before he'd pushed her up against a wall and kissed her until she was breathless and panting for more. They'd dated for roughly a month after that kiss and since their very brief relationship ended, she'd been nothing but 'Elizabeth' to him.

She mentally shook herself. Now wasn't the time to argue with him. The part of her that wanted to get as far away from Orlando Salas's house as possible knew that. She snatched the keys from his hand and hurried to his SUV. She might have a lot of questions for Porter, but more than anything she was simply grateful for his presence. If not for him, she'd probably be dead right now. Or worse. After what had just happened, energy hummed through her and she could actually feel her adrenaline high starting to crash. If he hadn't shown up when he had...Lizzy shivered and a cold sweat blossomed across her forehead. She couldn't think about that right now.

* * *

Raw, untamed energy hummed through Porter as he pulled away from the curb. He glanced once in the rearview mirror. It didn't look like they were being followed and so far Elizabeth's brother hadn't stirred.

Porter hated the distrust he'd seen in her eyes when he'd told her about the tracking device—something he'd hated putting on her car—but he'd had no choice. Not long ago her mother had called worried about her youngest son and his penchant to involve Elizabeth in his troubles. Since he'd seen firsthand what a destructive influence Benny had on Elizabeth, he hadn't hesitated to take things into his own hands. Putting a tracker in her car had been the only way he knew to discretely watch out for her.

If he could watch her all day he would. Though for a completely different reason than keeping her safe. The sexy woman had gotten under his skin in a bad way. Every night when he closed his eyes, he pictured her face. Her perfect smooth skin. Her perfect...everything. She was tall and slim and he often dreamed of running his hands through her mass of soft brown curls. And those espresso colored eyes were like dark pools just waiting to drown him. After their short relationship months ago, he'd forced himself to keep his distance. She'd made it perfectly clear that where her brother was concerned she had no common sense and that Porter would have no say in the decisions she made. Even decisions that could get her killed.

It didn't mean he could forget what it had been like to taste her. Right before they'd started dating, for a brief moment in her office he'd seen that white hot desire in her gaze. It had wrapped around him like a cocoon and threatened to suffocate him with its intensity. And he'd been willing to lose himself in her. So he'd kissed her. And she hadn't pushed him away. Until a month later when he'd tried to make her see reasoning that she couldn't keep bailing her brother out of trouble.

In the end he knew it was a good thing. She worked for his father's company and his brother was her boss. That kind of entanglement had disaster written all over it. And since it was clear he'd never be a priority in her life, it was better this way. There were too many things stacked against them and he wasn't a masochist.

As they neared her neighborhood, her brother started to stir. "Shit...where am I? Don't take me to the doctor. No hospitals..." he coughed out.

Porter glanced in the rearview mirror and glared. Dark eyes the same shade of brown as Elizabeth's stared at him with fear. "You're in the back of your sister's car. What the hell were you thinking dragging her down to Orlando Salas's house? What kind of moron are you?" Porter knew he should rein in his anger. This was her brother after all, but Orlando Salas was a dangerous predator. He preyed on women then spat them out like garbage. Now that Elizabeth was on that guy's radar, Porter was tempted to pack her up and haul her back to his place regardless of whether she wanted to go or not.

Shame filled Benny's eyes and he glanced away. "I didn't mean to get her involved in my troubles. I just...I needed help. I thought..." His voice broke on the last word.

Porter pushed back a twinge of guilt. The man had been beaten to a pulp so maybe he shouldn't be shouting at him. Still, there was no excuse in the world good enough for getting Elizabeth involved with Salas. "We're almost to your sister's place. What did you do to make Salas so angry?"

"I…uh, I owe him some money."

Porter was good at reading people. Benny Martinez definitely owed Salas money, but there was more he was keeping to himself. There was a stark, raw fear evident in his eyes and he wasn't trying to mask it. He apparently wore his heart on his sleeve, just like his sister.

Porter parked her car next to his SUV in the driveway and jumped out before Elizabeth had stopped the engine. He opened the back door and held an outstretched arm to Benny who was struggling to get out of his seat. "Come on."

Elizabeth hooked her arm under his other shoulder and propped Benny up. "Porter, you can leave now. I can handle it from here."

Porter snorted. That so wasn't going to happen. "Why don't you open the front door and I'll get him inside?" He'd formed it as a question, but he wasn't asking. After what had just happened, he wasn't letting her out of his sight.

It looked like she might argue but she snatched the keys from his outstretched hand and hurried up the short walkway. Her one-story bungalow-style home was tucked away behind a giant magnolia tree and a cluster of palmetto trees. She lived in a safe neighborhood, but safe was a relative word. After the potential enemy she'd just made, she was going to need his protection. Porter was more than willing to provide it.

The moment she opened the blue and white door, he sidestepped her, practically carrying Benny with him. "We need to figure out what to do with your brother. He doesn't want to go to a hospital but—"

"I think you should leave now." Her voice shook slightly but he ignored what it did to him. She sounded afraid and if he had to guess, embarrassed. Though he couldn't imagine why she'd be embarrassed. None of this was her fault. She'd been trying to help her brother. Even though he hated the way it obviously tore her up, he still admired her loyalty.

"Are you really going to fight me about this now? Your brother needs help."

Sighing, she shut and locked the door behind them and pointed straight ahead. "Kitchen's this way."

In the brief time they'd dated he'd never been to her place since she'd wanted to take things slow, but the cozy home fit her. Picture frames of various sizes dotted the wall along the short hallway leading to the other room. She pushed open the swinging white door to the kitchen and propped it open. Quickly she grabbed the vase of bright flowers in the middle of her table and moved it to one of the counters. "Lay him on the table."

Her brother groaned but didn't protest as Porter stretched him out onto the rectangular wooden table. At least he was conscious. If he hadn't been, they'd be on their way to the ER.

"Do you have a first aid kit?" he asked her.

Wordlessly she nodded and disappeared from the room. When she did, he found a pair of scissors in one of the drawers and cut Benny's already ripped polo shirt away from his body. The sides of his waist and stomach were bruised, but nothing looked fatal. And he'd have a serious shiner for the next week but unless he'd sustained internal injuries, he likely only had a few broken ribs. They'd hurt but they'd heal. If Orlando had beaten him because Benny owed him money, he wouldn't want the guy dead. Just in enough pain that he knew how bad it would be if he didn't come up with what he owed.

"We need to take him to a hospital," Elizabeth said as she strode back into the room. She handed Porter a basic first aid kit.

"No hospitals," Benny's voice was strong.

Porter ignored him. "Help me lift him up to a sitting position."

When she did, he pressed his fingers against Benny's ribcage.

"Ahh, what are you doing?" Benny moaned.

"Your ribs are probably cracked, maybe broken. You're going to need to see a doctor, get X-rays, but until then, I'm going to wrap this around you." Porter held up the elastic bandage.

Her brother nodded. "Okay."

"Can you hold him still while I wrap him?" he asked Elizabeth.

She bit her bottom lip, but nodded and slid her arm up under Benny's shoulders.

"I'm not going to wrap this too tight, Benny. You need to be able to breathe so tell me if you feel too much pressure." When Benny grunted, Porter continued talking. Elizabeth's brother didn't seem like he was close to going into shock but Porter wanted to keep him lucid. While he'd prefer to take him to the hospital, Porter could tell it would only cause Benny to fight them, and that was the last thing Elizabeth needed right now. "There's only so much we can do here. If one of your ribs is broken, it could puncture your lung or possibly your aorta."

Elizabeth sucked in a ragged breath beside him. "Benny, you *need* to see a doctor."

He shook his head. "No way. I can't...I can't stay here either. Gotta get out of here." He tried to struggle but slumped against his sister. "I just need to rest and I'll be fine," he mumbled.

After grabbing a bag of frozen peas from Elizabeth's freezer, he lifted Benny up. "Do you have a guest bedroom or somewhere you want to lay him?"

She nodded jerkily and motioned behind her. "Follow me."

His boots thumped lightly against the wood flooring as he trailed after her down a short hallway off the kitchen. There were two open doors on the right side of the hallway. The first opened into an office. She bypassed it and ducked into the second one. When he entered carrying her brother, she was pulling the light green and white flowered comforter back.

"Do you want to lay towels or something down? I still need to clean off some of his blood."

"I don't care about the sheets, Porter," she said softly.

Of course it was the wrong time, wrong place, wrong everything, but his heart jumped when she said his name. It always had. Probably because he always imagined her saying it under much different circumstances. Naked ones.

Wordlessly, he stretched her brother out. While he did, he was aware of Elizabeth leaving the room, but he continued inspecting the rest of Benny's wounds.

From what he could tell, time and sleep were the only things that would heal him and until he decided to go to a doctor, there wasn't much anyone else could do. At least the makeshift ice pack would help with the swelling on Benny's eye. Once Porter cleaned and bandaged Benny's face and arms, he tucked the covers around him and went in search of Elizabeth.

Whether she liked it or not, he wasn't leaving her side.

* * *

Lizzy smoothed her hands down the front of her dress. Why couldn't Porter just leave? While she really appreciated what he'd done for her—probably more than she'd ever be able to put into words—he was the last person in the world she wanted to witness her family drama. It was too embarrassing. Especially when his family was so normal.

After their break up she'd been able to deal with him ignoring her. At least then it was easier to keep things professional. Of course it hadn't done anything to quell her fantasies of him. Maybe if they'd actually had sex she'd be over him. It was just the unknown physical aspect she was drawn to because their personalities were way too different for anything long term to ever work out. That's what she kept trying to tell herself anyway.

Now she felt lost. She couldn't wrap her mind around the fact that he'd put a tracker in her car. It made no sense. It's not as if she was a bad employee. Even though things had never taken off between them she'd always thought he still respected her.

When he entered the kitchen, she wrapped her arms around herself and took a step back, bumping into the counter. His pale blue eyes always seemed to see right inside her, as if he knew what she was thinking. That every time she saw him all she wondered was what he'd look like completely naked. But that wasn't important now especially since it was never going to happen. "Why do you have a tracker in my car?"

"Your mother called not long ago worried about Benny. She said he had a tendency to bring you down with him..." He paused and she cringed at the judgment in his voice. "She wanted to know if I could keep an eye on you."

Her face flamed at his words. She was twenty-five, had a PhD in computer science and a really good job despite what her parents thought of her chosen profession. *And her mother was calling people she worked with like she was an irresponsible teenager?* Lizzy knew that even with her slightly darker coloring her face had to be bright red at the moment. "So that's the only reason?"

He cleared his throat and for the first time since she'd met him, he looked angry. At her. "She told me that a few years ago you picked your brother up from one of the southwest *barrios* and almost got *assaulted*. Why didn't you tell me about that when we were together?"

Now the color drained from her face and instead of heat, cold snaked through her body. Everything she'd ever wanted to keep private—especially from Porter, someone she was insanely attracted to—was now apparently common knowledge. Assaulted was a civilized way of putting what had happened. She'd almost been gang raped by a vicious bunch of meth addicts coming down from their high. The police avoided most of the southwest *barrios* but there had been a big enough disturbance the day they'd been there. If it hadn't been for the overwhelming police presence, she'd be dead. "It wasn't my brother's fault."

"Whose fault was it then? Do you frequent crack dens and meth houses on a regular basis?" His voice was soft but there was an underlying edge to it. Something told her it wasn't directed at her though, but her brother.

Everyone in her family judged Benny. She couldn't take it from Porter too. Not when Benny had always been there for her. Her family might want to brush their history under the rug but she wouldn't when it came to her brother. When she'd been twelve and he'd been barely fourteen, he'd stood up for her and had saved her from the worst possible thing any child should ever have to go through. "You don't know anything about my brother or my family," she snapped.

His blue eyes flashed angrily. "You're right, I don't. The only thing I know is that I would *never* knowingly put one of my family members in danger. I'd rather die first. I also know that when we were together, anytime he called, you jumped, night or day, ready to run into the worst situation to save him. Or loan him money. Your brother needs help but *you* can't give it to him. He needs to *want* to get help and all you're doing is enabling him. The sooner you realize that, the better."

"You need to leave." Her throat was tight and her voice unsteady. If she was in his presence any longer she was going to break down. She'd been getting Benny out of trouble for longer than she cared to admit. Having Porter see her at her worst was the last thing she could handle right now.

He snorted and took a few more steps into the room. "You just pissed off *Orlando Salas* and now you're on his radar. If I thought you'd listen, I'd pack you a bag and get you the hell out of here. Since I know that isn't going to happen, I'm staying."

"What do you mean, *staying?*" She felt stupid after asking since it was pretty obvious what he meant, but she was a little more than shaky. Since things had never progressed to a sexual level between them he'd never stayed at her house. The thought of him doing so now frightened her on too many levels.

One of his dark eyebrows arched. "I'm sleeping on your couch tonight darlin' so get used to it."

Darlin'. The word sounded far too intimate for the kind of relationship they had. Which was essentially nothing. An unexpected vision of him stretched out naked in her bed flashed before her eyes and she nearly gasped aloud. *Where had that come from?* Okay, it wasn't much of a surprise. She'd been fantasizing about him since before that first toe-numbing kiss they'd shared. Right now she couldn't help but wonder what he'd look like stripped out of the stuffy suit he wore. He was a good six inches taller than her and considering she was five foot eight, that was saying something. His broad shoulders simply begged for her to run her fingers over them. To clutch on to.

Sighing, she nodded instead of attempting to argue. By the firm set of his jaw she knew that no matter what she said, he'd stay. Even if she managed to kick him out, he'd sleep in his vehicle. If she was being honest with herself, she was glad he wanted to stick around. After the way Orlando had manhandled her, she was shaken up and Porter's presence was reassuring. On a personal level he might put her on edge but that was just a physical reaction. "I'll grab an extra pillow and blankets. Just don't expect me to cook dinner for you." Completely offending her mother's Cuban sensibilities, Lizzy had never picked up the knack for cooking.

"How about I cook for you instead?" The low baritone of his voice sent a shiver curling through her until it settled low in her belly.

Her eyes widened in surprise. *He could cook?* Something she hadn't known about him. She definitely needed to get away from this man. "Uh, sure, but I'm going to take a shower first," she muttered and skirted past him. She was careful not to touch him though. Touching him sent her senses haywire and turned her brain to mush. He was only going to be here one night anyway. She could manage to avoid him for a few hours and tomorrow her life would return to normal. She'd make sure of it.

CHAPTER TWO

Lizzy opened her eyes and sat straight up in bed as she heard a low creak from somewhere in her house. Her heart pounded wildly against her chest as she eased out of bed. Something felt...off. She didn't know what it was, but could feel it straight to her bones.

Her house had been built in the fifties so it was always making settling sounds. The noise she'd just heard could be nothing but she wasn't taking the chance.

Porter was sleeping on her couch and Benny was still in her guest room. She'd checked on her brother an hour ago and he'd looked a lot better than he had when they'd brought him home. A lot of the swelling on his face had gone down.

She tiptoed across her room and cringed when the floorboards groaned beneath her. Easing the door open, she peeked out to find the hallway empty. Good. Porter must still be asleep. She nudged the half-open door to the guest room all the way open. Her throat clenched at the empty bed. The sheets were rumpled but Benny wasn't there. He always did this. Just left without saying goodbye. She should be used to it, but it hurt more than she'd admit. When she felt wetness on her cheek, she brushed away a few stray tears that managed to leak out.

"He left fifteen minutes ago."

She swiveled at Porter's voice and barely refrained from screaming. Her hand instinctively flew to her throat. "You almost gave me a heart attack... You saw him leave?"

Porter nodded, his face an unreadable mask. "He must have called someone to pick him up because he snuck out the front door. I watched him get into a car and drive off."

Anger punched through her, swift and hard even though it had nothing to do with the man standing in front of her. This wasn't his fault. "Why didn't you try to stop him? Or wake me up?"

His shoulders lifted in a casual shrug. "He's a grown man. If he wants to leave, it's not my business."

She started to respond when she realized how little clothing Porter had on. No shirt and pinstriped blue and white boxers that did little to cover the bulge between his legs. *Oh my...* She forced her gaze upward but his entire body was drool worthy and she couldn't stop her gaze from roaming everywhere.

His broad chest was male perfection. With a ripped eight pack and just a smattering of dark hair covering his pecs, he was all sharp lines and taut muscles. She'd never thought much about male legs before, but his were something she'd definitely remember. Muscular and lean but not bulky. Runner's legs. Why had they never gotten naked together again? Right now she was having a hard time remembering her own name, let alone why she'd ended things with him. She nervously licked her lips as she imagined what it would be like to wrap her own legs around—

"Don't look at me like that." His voice was a low growl.

As her eyes snapped up to meet his, she fought the heat creeping into her cheeks. Thankfully the only source of illumination was the moonlight streaming in from the blinds. She wondered how long she'd been staring at him like he was a slab of meat. "Like what?" she whispered. Immediately she wanted to take the question back. It was lame and she knew exactly what she'd been doing. She'd been undressing him with her eyes and she was only sorry he'd stopped her.

He reached out and tucked a wayward curl behind her ear. Instead of withdrawing his hand, he cupped her cheek.

"Lizzy," he softly breathed out her name.

Her lips parted when his pale gaze zeroed in on her mouth. Porter was always so careful about not touching her since they'd ended things, but now he wasn't showing that normal restraint. When he didn't pull away, it was like a switch flipped inside her. She wanted his touch so bad she ached for it. For months they'd been dancing around their still burning attraction for one another and he'd just lit the pilot light on her desire. If he didn't kiss her, she was going to scream in frustration.

He muttered something unintelligible and covered her mouth with his lightning fast as if he was afraid she'd change her mind. His kiss was soft, yet somehow still demanding. He coaxed her mouth open until their tongues were hungrily clashing against each other. She'd missed his taste so much. When he pulled her bottom lip between his teeth, she didn't bother to hide her moan. She'd never stopped wanting him. Wanting what he always made her feel.

He threaded his fingers through her hair and held the back of her head in a dominating grip. The pressure was just enough to drive her wild. She clutched his shoulders and held on tight, savoring the feel of all that strength and power under her fingertips.

When he pulled back she felt the loss immediately but he wasn't going anywhere. He dipped his head and feathered light, sensuous kisses along her jaw until he reached her earlobe. Just like he knew was guaranteed to drive her crazy. "I want you so bad, Lizzy."

There he went with her nickname again. His voice softened and his eyes darkened every time he said it. And like magic, heat pooled deep in her belly each time.

She couldn't see his eyes at the moment but the man's voice was the strongest aphrodisiac. Potent and intoxicating. If she could bottle it up she would.

She opened her mouth to tell him she felt the same way when loud staccato pops somewhere outside made her jerk back. In a haze, she stared at him. "What—"

His expression was tense. "Stay here!"

Porter turned and sprinted back down the hallway. Instead of doing as he said, she hurried after him. When he grabbed his gun from the coffee table in her living room, she realized what he was doing.

"Stay down," he threw over his shoulder as he neared the window.

Crouching low, she peered around the corner of the couch and watched as he slowly lifted one of the wooden slat blinds covering the window in her living room. Fear for whatever was going on outside exploded inside her like fireworks. But more than anything, she wanted to pull Porter down to where she was. She had no doubt he could take care of himself but that didn't ease her panic any. The back of her neck tingled as he stood off to the side of her window. It sounded like gunfire outside though she couldn't wrap her mind around something like that happening in her quiet neighborhood. Maybe it was just some kids lighting fireworks.

Porter muttered a curse under his breath.

The pops sounded again and they were followed by loud shouts and whoops. The noise grew farther and farther away, but her heart still pounded erratically. "What is that?"

He moved away from the window and grabbed his neatly folded jeans from the coffee table and started to tug them on. "You need to pack a bag. For at least two weeks."

She cautiously crept up from behind her hiding place. "What's going on?"

"Someone just made a mess of your lawn and shot off a few rounds overhead—probably to make sure you woke up to see what they were doing. We're lucky they didn't aim at your house," he growled.

"What did they do to my lawn?" An unbidden tremor raced through her voice.

"See for yourself." He motioned with his head as he zipped and buttoned his jeans.

Fighting panic, she headed toward the window and lifted one of the wooden slats a fraction. Her heart caught in her throat. Someone had burned something into her front yard. Burning orange embers danced and floated under the moonlight. "What is that? It looks like numbers. Why would someone burn numbers into my yard?"

Porter wrapped his arm around her waist from behind and pulled her away from the window. She nearly jumped out of her skin. Despite the fear humming through her, she enjoyed the intimacy of the way he held her. Turning, she faced him and didn't move out of his embrace. The rational part of her brain told her to move away but instead, she wrapped her arms around him. Screw rational. Right now she needed that extra bit of strength.

He tugged her completely away from the window and into the shadows of the living room. "Those numbers mean you've made a serious enemy, Lizzy. It's a seventy-nine." His tone was so dark and ominous and he made the statement with such finality, as if she should have any sort of clue what he meant.

"And...what? I've got seventy-nine days to live?" She tried to sound light but her question came out raspy.

"It's a message from the Seventy-Ninth Street Gang. They used to do a lot of low level work for Alberto Salas before he died. Looks like they're working for his son, Orlando, too."

"Why would they or he come after me?" She might have made him angry earlier today but her brother owed Orlando money, not her.

Porter's face was a virtual mask. "This is probably about your brother. He could be trying to threaten you in order to get Benny to pay whatever he owes. Or maybe I made Orlando angry by knocking him out and he feels like he needs to save face in front of his men. I don't know enough about Orlando to know the answer. Either way, I'm keeping you under lockdown until we have a better idea what his intentions are."

"How do you even know what that number means? It could mean—"

"Grant works for the Miami PD and he's done a lot of undercover work with the local gang task force. I *know* what that number means and it's a message. This is just a warning. You don't want to be around when they come back."

She'd forgotten his other brother was a cop. "Shouldn't we call the police then?"

He nodded. "While you're packing I'll call Grant. He's a detective now. You can make a statement to him later and he can have someone head down here to document your front yard. I don't want to stick around in case these guys decide to make another visit tonight."

That was fine with her. The more reality set in, she didn't want to hang around her house either. And she hated that. Her home was her safe haven and now she felt violated. She wiped sweaty palms against her pajama pants as she stepped out of his embrace. "I'll go pack." As she passed the guestroom, she paused when she saw a folded piece of paper on the nightstand.

She hurried toward it and picked it up. Glancing over her shoulder, she sighed when she realized Porter hadn't followed her. Her hands trembled as she unfolded it. It was Benny's handwriting.

I'm so sorry, hermana. I'm a coward to leave in the middle of the night but I'm too ashamed to face you in the morning. For the first time in months everything is clear. Next time I call you asking for help, I beg you not to do it. I'm so ashamed I asked you to Orlando's house knowing what a monster he is. I don't deserve a sister like you and I'm sorry for all the trouble I've caused you. I've done something stupid but I needed insurance. Orlando doesn't know what I've done yet but he will soon enough. My insurance will keep you alive. I left it for you in our childhood hiding place. You'll know what to do. Don't trust anyone with what I'm giving you. Te quiero, Benito.

Insurance? What did that mean? And what could he have left for her?

"Elizabeth?" Porter's voice trailed down the hall.

Fighting back the sting of tears, she crumpled the paper and hurried to her room. There would be time enough later to figure out what kind of trouble her brother was in. She didn't care what Benny said, she could never abandon her brother.

* * *

Orlando stared at the picture of Elizabeth Martinez on his computer screen. Everything about her was perfect. She came from a respected family, she was well-liked around Miami, and she was beautiful. Not in a showy, trashy sort of way, but elegant and refined. Exactly what his family wasn't. And exactly what he wanted in a wife.

He'd made a mistake yesterday by striking her, but he'd finally gotten her right where he wanted her and he'd lost control. At every function he'd ever spoken to Elizabeth, she'd been a quiet little thing and he hadn't expected her to fight him. It had taken months to get her brother, Benito, in a position to owe him money. Orlando had wanted to push him into a corner and force the man to call Elizabeth and beg for help. After that time and planning everything had gone to shit in seconds.

And all because of Porter Caldwell. Orlando hadn't recognized the guy until it was too late. Porter's involvement with Elizabeth put a wrinkle in his plans.

He'd known she worked for the Caldwell family but hadn't realized the apparent extent of her relationship with them. If it had been *anyone* else, he'd simply kill them and be done with it. But if he had a member of the Caldwell family executed, it would surely fall back on his doorstep ten-fold. Porter's family had ties with almost every branch of the government—and he was pretty sure Porter's father was a retired spy if the rumors around the city were true. Orlando didn't need that kind of heat.

Despite the fact that growing up his father had always told him what a screw-up he was, Orlando wasn't stupid and he certainly didn't have a death wish. No, he'd have to deal with Porter another way. More subtly.

A sharp knock on his office door jerked him out of his thoughts. Frowning, he glanced at the clock. It was barely five and the sun hadn't yet risen. There was only one person who would be up as early as he.

He clicked off Elizabeth's picture and pulled up a spreadsheet. "Come in."

Miguel, his cousin and one of the few people in the world he trusted, stepped in. His dark eyebrows pulled together in concern. "Hey, you busy?"

Orlando shook his head. "What's up?"

Miguel cleared his throat. "I just got a call from Juan."

"And?" Orlando had sent Juan and Eddie, two members of the Seventy Ninth Street Gang, over to scare Elizabeth at her house. If he hadn't been sure that Porter would be there, he might have had them do more than scare her, but he couldn't risk Porter getting hurt in the crossfire. Not yet anyway.

"Looks like it worked. They did as you asked. Currently her car's still there but it looks like she's cleared out."

"Good." He'd expected her to leave. If she was scared she'd be more amendable to listening to him next time. He had eyes all over Miami and he knew exactly where she worked. Even if she stayed in hiding, all he'd have to do was follow her home from work one day. Well, he'd have one of his men do it.

He needed her terrified of him, to realize that she had no other choice but to listen to his demands. From what he knew about Elizabeth, she was loyal to a fault to her brother and Benny's debt wasn't going to go away anytime soon. He needed to convince her to pay off her brother's debt with herself. Yes, he'd have to scare her again very soon. If he let too much time lapse between what the gang had done tonight and another incident, it wouldn't make as much of an impact.

When Orlando's cousin didn't make a move to leave, he arched an eyebrow. "Is there something else?"

Miguel cleared his throat again, a definite sign he was nervous. "I don't understand why you're using our manpower for something as trivial as a hundred K. With our new product, it doesn't make sense to focus on this. We should just kill Benny and make him an example. Why not leave the sister alone?"

"Since when do you question my decisions?" Orlando didn't understand his cousin's view toward the opposite sex. Women were nothing more than entertainment—or trophies to display—but for some reason Miguel had a soft spot for women. He knew that was the real reason Miguel wanted him to back off from scaring Elizabeth.

His cousin held up his hands in a placating gesture. "You're right, I'm sorry." He quickly backpedaled and shut the door behind him.

Sighing, Orlando sat back in front of his computer and pulled up another picture of Elizabeth. Need burned deep inside him as he stared at her. Her head was thrown back and she was laughing at something her mother had said. All that dark hair of hers spilled around her face and shoulders. The woman looked like a goddess. The picture was from a charity function for animals or some other crap. He might not remember the reason for the event, but he remembered everything about her from that night. She'd only had two glasses of champagne before switching to water, and every time she'd moved, her long black dress had swayed seductively, showing him peeks of her mile-long legs. She was a tall woman, especially for being Cuban, and her body was her best asset. Well that and her family name.

He'd tried to talk to her, but she'd been surrounded by her family. Her two oldest brothers hadn't left her side the entire night. They'd been like rabid guard dogs, baring their teeth to anyone who got too close. But he'd find a way to get to her. It was all about timing. One way or another, Elizabeth was going to be his. Her family was highly respected in the Miami circuit and he needed that clout. He might have money but his father had never made an attempt to gain any respect around town. No, all he'd cared about was people fearing him.

Fear was important to Orlando too, but he didn't want a life like his father's. He wanted someone classy like Elizabeth to be his. Not some trashy dancer like his father had married. Orlando's lip curled up as he thought about his dead mother. Good riddance to both his parents. His life was going to be much different than his father's. He'd make sure of it.

CHAPTER THREE

Porter tried calling his brother again, impatient as he waited for Grant to pick up. He'd gotten in touch with him last night and Grant had sent a uniform over to document Elizabeth's yard. He'd wanted her to come down to the station but Porter had been adamant that she make a statement later. The time lag wouldn't make a difference since they knew who'd left that insignia in her yard. Leaving a calling card wasn't exactly a genius move.

Next he'd called his other brother, Harrison, and told him that Elizabeth wouldn't be coming to work—though he expected her to fight him on that. That was too bad.

Now he needed more info from Grant so he could figure out how best to protect Lizzy. After eight years in the Marines and the six after that spent protecting people, he had a lot of training and experience when it came to security situations and he wanted to know as much about this enemy as possible. Any edge he had to keep Elizabeth safe.

Grant answered on the second ring. "Hey, I was just about to call you back."

"What do you know?"

"Good morning to you too." Grant's voice was wry.

Porter didn't bother with niceties or an apology. Right now he was too wired. "I've got a lot on my mind."

"I know, man. We're going to keep Lizzy safe. Has she been able to tell you anything else?"

Porter ignored the twinge of annoyance by his brother's use of Elizabeth's nickname. So far everyone in his family was at perfect ease around her. She'd been working for Red Stone Security for the past couple years, and hell, she was the best friend of Harrison's fiancé. If it hadn't been for all the security jobs he'd taken around the globe the past couple years, he'd have met her in person long ago. Instead he'd only met her face to face months ago and he hadn't been able to get her out of his mind since. He *should* feel comfortable around her and he hated that he always seemed to be edgy in her presence. "No, but she's still sleeping. Didn't want to wake her yet. And you know everything I know. Her youngest brother seems to have gotten into trouble with Orlando Salas and now Elizabeth is being targeted by the Seventy Ninth Street Gang." Porter guessed to give Benny more of an incentive to pay up. Going after Benny through Elizabeth was actually smart. The Martinez family might have washed their hands of Benny but they'd never let anything happen to their daughter.

Grant cursed. "This gang's been a thorn in my side for years. If we can bring them *and* Salas down it'll be big for the department and the city. You gonna keep Lizzy at your place today?"

As if he'd let her go anywhere. "Of course. I have a meeting in a few hours but I'm going to work from home most of the day."

"I'll put out more feelers but I don't have anything new yet. I promise to call when I have something. You don't have to keep blowing up my phone," his brother said semi-jokingly.

Porter cringed. He'd been doing just that all morning but he felt so damn helpless. "I know."

"Let me know when she wakes up and we can set up a time for her to make an official report through me. I'll come to your place, bring some pictures of the gang members we have on file on the off-chance she recognizes one of them."

She hadn't seen anyone last night but Porter knew there was a chance she might remember seeing one of the gang members before. "Thanks." Once they disconnected he tossed the phone onto his kitchen counter and picked up his cup of coffee.

Right now he wished Benny was in front of him so he could wring his neck. It was obvious how much Elizabeth cared for her brother, and while her loyalty was commendable, it burned him up that Benny treated her like garbage. Benny called her for help or money and she went running to him regardless of how dangerous the situation. That wasn't happening anymore as long as Porter was around. He'd do everything in his power to protect her, but he had the feeling she wasn't going to make it easy for him.

Hell, if their past relationship was any indication she definitely wasn't. When they'd been dating he'd made a few comments about the trouble her brother always seemed to get into and she'd shut him down fast. Right now he could deal with the fact that her brother was important to her, but if she wanted to run headfirst into danger he wasn't letting her go alone.

* * *

The strong aroma of coffee rolled over Lizzy, forcing her eyes open. Inhaling deeply, she knew she couldn't stay in bed any longer. She threw the satiny blue comforter off her and slid out of the guest bed she'd slept in. Porter's condo in the high-rise building was definitely pricey, but the interior was a little sparse. It almost felt like a hotel. She'd been there a couple times and with the exception of the carpeted bedrooms, every other room had tile floors. Minimal decorations, a few family photos, a kitchen that looked as if it was never used and all the appliances looked brand new, as if he'd just taken them out of the box. After they'd arrived at his place last night he'd told her to get some sleep then had disappeared into his room. Unlike the times she'd been there before there had been no suggestion that they take things into his bedroom. It had felt weird to be here again under such different circumstances.

She'd hoped maybe they'd talk more about that kiss—or continue it—but Porter wasn't exactly known for his communication skills. Maybe it was a good thing he hadn't wanted to chat. Or do anything else. Because if he'd made a move on her, she'd have gone into his arms willingly and likely regretted it this morning when it was back to business as usual.

She dug her toes into the plush carpet before leaving her room to find him. The tiled hallway chilled her bare feet but the second she found Porter sitting at the center island of his kitchen sipping a cup of coffee and reading a newspaper, warmth flared deep inside her. It pushed out from her core, straight to all her nerve endings like an invisible flame lapping away at her insides.

He was already dressed in dark jeans, a polo shirt, and a sports coat. No suit for him today. She liked the change. Glancing down at her pink pajama pants and matching tank top, she bit her lip. Maybe she should have showered and changed first.

When he looked up at her, she froze, feeling like that clichéd deer in headlights. The absolutely primitive gaze he raked over her from head to feet had her nipples tightening under her top. She might as well be naked for how he made her feel so exposed, so *aware* of her body. Not wanting to draw attention to her physical reaction, she resisted the urge to cross her arms over her chest.

She cleared her throat and pointed at the coffee maker. "Got enough left for me?"

He nodded and his voice was slightly strangled as he said, "I've got milk in the fridge and that silver tin has sugar if you'd like."

"Thanks." Averting her gaze, she grabbed a mug

"Did you sleep all right?" he asked as she started to add a spoonful of sugar to her mug.

Not really. "Yes." She slid into the seat next to his, hyperaware of his spicy scent. She'd been wired after what had happened but the most primal part of her had known she was safe sleeping under his roof so she *should* have been able to rest. She'd tried to order her body to listen but thoughts of what it had felt like to have his lips on hers, had kept her wide awake.

"I don't have much in the way of food but I think I can scrounge up a bagel or toast." His expression was apologetic.

"That's okay." She wasn't a big breakfast person and as long as she got her coffee she was fine. She lightly tapped her finger against her mug as she tried to think of the right way to bring up last night. She'd always felt comfortable in her own skin except when she was around Porter. Even when they'd been dating she'd always felt on edge around him. As if there was some sort of electrical current between them that was almost tangible. "Listen, about last night..."

He shook his head. "Don't worry about anything. I already talked to Harrison and he doesn't have a problem with you not coming into work today, and Grant wants to talk to you personally so you can—"

"Wait, *what*? First of all, I'm not skipping work, but I do want to talk to Grant. And I wasn't talking about *that*. I thought maybe..." She trailed off, hating the way her cheeks heated up. Yeah, talking about that kiss probably wasn't the best idea. Obviously they were on two separate wavelengths. He was clearly more level headed than her. She was obsessing over it and he wanted to discuss what was actually important. She definitely needed to pull her head out of the clouds.

His pale eyes darkened as he scooted a fraction closer to her. "You shouldn't be out today."

"Why? Because some losers burned numbers into my lawn? I'm not going to live in fear. Besides, I work at one of the most secure buildings in Miami. I'd rather be there surrounded by people than cooped up here."

He sat his mug down with a thud. "Damn it, Lizzy—"

"Don't you 'Lizzy', me. You only use that name when you want something and it's not going to work this time." If he thought he could use her attraction to him *against* her, he was out of his mind.

She watched in fascination as a faint shade of red crept up his neck. "That's not true."

"Yes, it is. You always call me Elizabeth unless you're trying to charm me." *Or when you're kissing me.* She decided to keep that thought to herself though.

"I'm not trying to charm you," he muttered.

Her eyebrows rose. "Then what would you call it?"

"I'm trying to make you use common sense."

She snorted very loudly, earning a surprised look from him, but she didn't care. Pushing her chair back, she stood. "I'm not staying here and there's nothing you can say to make me change my mind. I'll go crazy so if you don't mind, I'm going to shower." Lizzy started to leave, but he grasped her upper arm.

Not hard, but he exerted enough pressure that she couldn't move.

She glared at him. "Let me go."

"You need to talk to Grant."

"I will, but it doesn't have to be here. I can meet him at the police station or he can come to my office or wherever."

"You'll be *safer* here," he ground out.

She dug her heels in but didn't say anything. He could argue until he was blue in the face. It wasn't as if he could hold her hostage.

At her lack of response, he practically growled at her. "Why do you have to be so stubborn?"

"Why do you always think you know what's best for me?" she shot back.

"You're the most frustrating woman I know." He let her arm drop and scrubbed a hand over his face. Without another word he moved past her and disappeared from the kitchen.

She stared at his retreating figure and frowned. Porter never let his guard down. *Ever.* But it seemed he was just as off-kilter in her presence as she was in his. The realization was strangely refreshing.

* * *

Lizzy glanced up as the handle to her office door jiggled. Before the door opened, she tensed. Porter had been so adamant that she not come into work this morning—an argument he'd most definitely lost—but she wouldn't put it past him to come here and try to convince her again to go back to his place.

The tension in Lizzy's shoulders relaxed when Carla Pickett, the receptionist for the eleventh floor, stepped halfway inside. "Hey, Lizzy, Mara's here. I figured it would be okay if she came back, but I wasn't sure if you were busy—"

She smiled and pressed the power button on her computer screen so it went dark. Her friend was a little early for their weekly lunch date but Lizzy had been working on security upgrades all morning and her brain was just about fried. "It's totally fine."

Mara was not only her boss's soon-to-be wife, she was Lizzy's best friend. Before she'd rounded the desk, Mara hurried into the room, an expression of pure panic on her face. "Harrison told me what happened. Are you all right? And why didn't you call me?"

Lizzy hadn't called her friend because she hadn't wanted to worry Mara. Better to deflect with another question. "Is Harrison with you?" His presence at the office had been scarce over the past couple weeks. He was still coming in to check up with the various teams of guys he oversaw, but he wasn't taking any direct security jobs due to his and Mara's upcoming wedding.

"No, he's working on... Don't change the subject. What's going on? And why did I hear it secondhand?" Mara shook her head as she pulled Lizzy into a tight hug.

"I honestly don't know what's going on. I think Benny might have gotten in a little over his head this time," she murmured as she stepped out of the embrace. That was an understatement considering how much he owed Salas. *One hundred thousand dollars.* If she knew how to get in contact with her brother she would, but the cell phone he'd called her from last time had already been disconnected. She needed to get to her parents' house to check out what he said he'd left for her in his note. First she'd need to convince Porter to take her there.

"A little? Porter told Harrison that a gang left their symbol burned into *your* front yard." Mara raked a hand through her short blond pixie cut.

"Yes, but I don't know why or even if it's connected to my brother." She didn't actually have any doubts but she didn't want to throw her brother under the bus.

"Well I certainly doubt they targeted you for any other reason," Mara shot back, her expression grim.

Lizzy knew that much was true but held back a response. She didn't want to talk about Benny's shortcomings now. Her brother had protected her when she was younger in a way her parents hadn't. If it hadn't been for him...she shuddered, not wanting to think about the past. "I'm supposed to talk to Grant later today and look at some mug shots—not that I think I'll recognize anyone—and I stayed at Porter's last night so please don't worry. Whatever is going on I'm sure we'll figure it out." If only she truly felt that way. Her insides quaked every time she thought about a gang knowing where she lived.

"Well at least lunch will be safe, and we're *not* staying here. Harrison has given me a freaking security detail. I swear, our wedding is making him more paranoid than usual."

Lizzy bit back a grin. Yeah, that definitely sounded like her boss. And right now she was thankful for his paranoia. She'd planned to eat downstairs in the cafeteria with Mara. When Porter dropped her off earlier this morning she'd promised she wouldn't leave the building, but if her boss thought it was okay then she supposed it was.

Lizzy smoothed her hands down her charcoal pencil skirt as they headed for the door. "Something sort of happened last night."

Her friend's green eyes narrowed knowingly. "With you and Porter? Did you guys finally—"

"Mara!" Lizzy glanced around but no one was anywhere near the elevators. When she looked back at her friend, she was smiling like she'd just won the lottery. Lizzy had told her about her short, sort-of fling—just without the sex—with Porter because she'd had to tell *someone*. That didn't mean she wanted the entire building to know. At the time she and Porter had made a deal to keep it quiet from everyone, namely his family, until they figured out if they even had a future. After they broke up she was very thankful she'd been insistent on secrecy.

She'd worked hard to earn a respected management position in the security department at Red Stone and she didn't want people to think she'd gotten it by sleeping around. Sure, she still answered to Harrison, but as a senior systems security manager, she had a lot of people who answered to her and she didn't want to lose their respect. Even though she'd been working at the company years before she'd even met Porter in person, it wouldn't matter. People talked and judged. "You didn't tell anyone about...us, right?"

Mara snorted loudly. "If you're asking if I told Harrison, the answer is *still* no. Your secret is safe, but you did stay at Porter's place last night so..." She trailed off, a silent question hanging in the air.

Lizzy sighed as they stepped into the open elevator. "We sort of kissed. But this morning he didn't want to talk about it." Which maybe wasn't such a bad idea. She could probably forget if he didn't stare at her with such raw heat in his eyes every time he glanced in her direction.

Her friend started to say something but Lizzy cut her off with a shake of her head. She couldn't start talking or thinking about Porter if she wanted to get anything done today. They had no future and she didn't need the distraction. Clearing her throat, Lizzy brushed away thoughts of him. "Sorry, I don't know why I even brought it up. Let's not talk about him anyway. Are you excited about tonight?" It was Mara's engagement dinner.

Mara's eyes lit up. "I am, mainly for the food though. Some famous caterer owed Harrison a favor so they agreed to handle the engagement party *and* the wedding reception. I don't think he cares either way who we use."

"Probably not. He'd be happy if you had a barbecue in your backyard." She'd worked for Harrison long enough to know that about him. The only time she'd ever seen him agonize over *anything* was when he'd been picking out an engagement ring. He'd do anything to make Mara happy.

"Truthfully, I don't care what we do either, but so far everything is going off without a hitch."

After the elevator doors whooshed open on the bottom floor, Lizzy paused when she saw four guys in suits waiting by the revolving glass doors. Fear snaked up her spine. She placed a light hand on Mara's arm and didn't make a move to get out. "Do you know those guys?"

"Yeah, that's the team Harrison ordered to watch out for us today."

"*Four* extra guys?"

Mara shrugged as they exited the elevator. "Yep."

Lizzy tried to squash her nerves as she followed her friend into the lobby. Maybe they should just eat in the cafeteria. One of the men looked familiar, but she didn't recognize the other three. Harrison oversaw about forty men, and while she interacted with them on a semi-regular basis, they had a couple hundred guys working for the company, some of whom she'd never met. She wasn't worried that they wouldn't be competent, but the thought of actually needing a security detail for her own protection freaked her out.

She couldn't imagine some low-life gang members targeting her in broad daylight in the middle of the financial district. She hadn't done anything anyway. Orlando hadn't seemed like he wanted to kill her. No, he'd had something else in mind for her. And why would he want her dead? She'd always thought he was a bit of a psychopath but killing her would be pointless. Still…seeing these men in front of her put her on edge.

"You sure you're all right?" Mara's quiet voice startled her out of her thoughts as they stepped outside.

Instead of voicing her worries, she pasted on a bright smile and nodded. "Of course, I'm just starving."

Two of the men went through the revolving door before them and two flanked them from behind. These guys were no joke. All of her work was at a computer and she'd never actually seen any of the security teams in action before, but they seemed to know what they were doing.

There was a white SUV with tinted windows waiting directly outside for them. And if she knew her boss the vehicle was bullet proof. "This is our ride?" she asked Mara.

"Yep. It's one of Harrison's newest armored vehicles and—"

Her words were cut off when one of the men grabbed her arm and started hustling them faster. "Ladies, you need to get into the SUV, *now*."

As they rushed toward the open door, Lizzy spotted a shiny blue two-door muscle car screech to a halt across the street from them. The door flew open and two men wearing blue bandanas across their face and carrying what looked like machine guns jumped out. Panic slammed into her chest. "Hey!" She pointed, but one of the security guys practically picked her up and shoved her through the open vehicle door.

Mara tumbled in behind her, pinning her on the floor, and a second later, like hail on a tin roof, there was an explosion of gunfire all around them. The staccato pings were deafening and seemed to go on forever. Thank God the SUV was armored.

Lizzy's heart pounded loudly in her ears but nothing could drown out the outside noise. Mara huddled half on top of her and she was vaguely aware of the men shouting something. What though, she had no clue.

When the vehicle jerked to life, the sounds of shooting miraculously faded then stopped all together. Lizzy's eyes flew open with a start—she hadn't realized they'd been closed—to find Mara still on top of her. Her friend pushed up and sat on the middle of the bench seat as she helped Lizzy slide up next to her. Straightening, she stared at her friend, then glanced around.

The driver and man in the passenger seat were silent, but the man sitting next to them was quietly talking into his phone. She didn't know who was on the other end, but she could guess as she listened to his half of the conversation.

"...already called the cops...the women are secure...two guys from what we could see...Tony got cover inside and stayed back to try and follow them..."

"Are you okay?" she whispered to Mara.

"I'm fine." Mara nodded and Lizzy was surprised by how stoic she appeared. Not a hair was out of place and her sharp, Slavic features didn't betray an ounce of emotion. She looked perfectly at ease. No wonder she and Harrison fit together so perfectly.

"That was insane! How can you be fine?" Lizzy felt as if her insides were actually shaking. A slight tremor rolled over her and she was helpless to stop it. She clasped her hands tightly in her lap to calm them but it did no good.

Mara's eyebrows rose in concern and she immediately covered Lizzy's hands in a reassuring grip. "I'm scared too, but we're alive, okay? They're taking us somewhere safe, I promise."

Lizzy nodded and internally berated herself for the tears she felt rising up. If Mara was okay, she supposed she should suck it up too. But she obviously wasn't wired like her friend. Men with guns trying to shoot them in the middle of the day? She quickly glanced out the window, but everything blurred before her. Keeping her face turned away, she tried to blink away the hot tears threatening to spill down her cheeks. She wasn't going to ask, mainly because she didn't trust her voice, but she really hoped that wherever they were going, Porter would be there too.

CHAPTER FOUR

Porter slipped his sunglasses on as he exited the Hotel Victor. A potential client had picked the place to meet and all he'd thought about the entire time was that the Parisian style hotel would be a nice place to take Elizabeth to dinner. It seemed everywhere he went the gorgeous woman occupied his thoughts. If he hadn't known she was safe at the office he wouldn't have even gone to the meeting.

His cell buzzed in his pocket. As he answered it, he handed his parking stub to one of the valet guys. When he saw Harrison's number, he smiled. "Hey man, the meeting went well. I think we just landed the entire Mancini corporate account."

"That's not why I'm calling."

His heart stuttered at his brother's grim tone. "Elizabeth." Her name was all he could squeeze out. If something had happened to her—

"She's fine but there was an incident."

He practically shoved the valet driver out of the way after he'd put Porter's vehicle in park. "Where is she?"

"My house."

If he took a couple shortcuts he could be at Harrison's in twenty minutes. "Tell me what happened."

"A couple gangbangers opened fire on them right outside of Red Stone." Now there was an unmistakable edge to his brother's voice.

Someone had taken a shot at her? A low buzz started in Porter's ears as he felt himself slip into battle mode. Even as he kept a lid on his emotions, his stomach twisted at the thought of anything happening to Lizzy. Gripping the wheel tightly, he took a sharp turn. "What was she even doing outside? She wasn't supposed to leave the building!"

"I know. She and Mara were going to lunch with a *full* security team and—"

"You're *sure* it was from a gang?" Porter cut him off. He didn't care why she'd left the building and he wasn't going to waste his breath arguing about how stupid it had been. All he cared about was that she was safe.

"They fit the profile. One of my guys got the license plate and I already had Grant run it—it doesn't exist."

Which meant someone had likely taken two halves of different plates and welded them together. A common practice among car thieves and gang members in Miami. Before Porter could respond, Harrison continued.

"For now Lizzy's at my place with Mara. We need to talk to her because after this I think she might know more than she's telling. I don't see why Salas would send a gang after her in broad daylight, not over money her brother owes him. Doesn't make sense."

It didn't. Especially not considering who Porter's family was. Orlando Salas couldn't be that stupid. "I'll see you in a few." He disconnected and shoved the phone in his pocket.

Time seemed to move backward as he maneuvered through traffic, but the drive was relatively short. When he pulled up to his brother's spacious two story home in the quiet Coral Gables neighborhood, he wasn't surprised to see a team of guys parked in the driveway and another parked across the street. He was certain there would be more men inside. Everything about Harrison's life was low-key, right down to the ten-year-old Ford truck he drove—though it did have bullet resistant glass windows. But if there was a potential threat anywhere near Mara, he was anything but laid back.

Porter completely understood. He wanted to keep Elizabeth under lock and key so no one could hurt her. Before he'd reached the front door, it flew open.

Harrison stood back and motioned for him to enter. "She's in the living room."

He brushed past his brother until he reached the archway that opened into the living room. Wearing the same button down pink top and slim-fitting skirt she'd had on that morning, she sat with her legs crossed and her hands clasped tightly over her knees. The whites of her knuckles were a stark contrast to her naturally tanned skin.

She glanced up and when those espresso colored eyes of hers locked on his, it was like a punch to the gut. Unlike his brother's fiancé, who was as cool as ice under any circumstance, Elizabeth was more innocent. Sweeter and softer. And right now she looked so damn vulnerable. She spent her days behind a computer and if he had to guess, she'd grown up fairly sheltered. Her parents were two of the highest paid doctors on the East Coast, or more likely the country. One was a cardiologist and the other an oncologist. Combined with the events of yesterday, having a couple thugs try to gun her down had probably shaken her up more than she was letting on.

When he moved into the room, she stood and skirted around the coffee table toward him. "I'm sorry, I should have listened to you and stayed home today. I..."

Her voice broke and he covered the rest of the distance in two strides. Surprising himself, he pulled her into a tight hug. He didn't care what his brother thought about his display of affection for her. For a split second she was resistant but then her slim arms wrapped around him and held tight. Her head fit right under his chin. She was so close he could feel the rapid beat of her heart and the soft swell of her breasts pressing against his chest. The way she hitched in a breath made him ache inside.

"If I'd listened to you, none of this would have happened." There was a slight note of anger in her words. Anger at herself, he guessed.

He squeezed her tighter, needing to feel her against him. "If I'd thought this was remotely possible, I wouldn't have let you go to work today. You couldn't have seen this coming. Neither of us could have," he murmured against her hair. She was fairly tall, but today she felt soft and fragile in his arms. Without caring about the consequences, he brushed a hand down her long hair and smoothed it down her spine. He was so grateful she was unharmed and letting him hold her. Feeling her like this kept him grounded and reminded him she was okay. It also let him breathe normally.

The longer he held her, the more he savored the way her soft curves pressed against him in all the right places. The timing was inappropriate but his lower body came to life with a roar. He became aware of it only seconds before she did. She pulled her head back, away from his chest, but didn't step out of his embrace. Her dark eyes widened and she opened her mouth to speak, but the sound of his brother clearing his throat brought them back to reality. Instantly they broke apart and not a second too soon. Porter needed to get his shit together around her.

"We need to talk," Harrison said as he stepped fully into the room, giving Porter a curious look.

Porter nodded and took Elizabeth's hand as he sat on the longer leather couch, pulling her with him. She looked surprised by the gesture, but he had to touch her. He noticed Mara wasn't in the room, but he didn't ask questions. If Harrison didn't think she needed to be there, then she didn't.

"What do you guys want to know?" she asked as she looked back and forth between them.

"Do you have any idea what kind of trouble your brother could have gotten into?" Harrison spoke first.

For a moment, something flashed in her dark gaze, but it was gone so quick he didn't have time to analyze it. She shook her head. "I know he owes Orlando money, but I don't know why Orlando would want to kill *me* because of that. The attack today doesn't make any sense."

"Is there anything else you can think of that happened while you were at his house? Something your brother said to you, maybe. Or something Orlando said to you? Maybe you saw something Orlando doesn't want you to repeat to anyone?" Porter asked.

Nervously, she cleared her throat and averted her gaze. She stared at his chest instead of his face. He didn't think she was trying to hide anything but she looked uncomfortable. As if she didn't want to say what was on her mind. Finally she broke the silence. "Orlando said...he'd take what my brother owed him from me in a, uh...I'm pretty sure he meant a sexual manner."

For a moment blood roared in Porter's ears like a raging angry river.

"He said if I was 'his' for six months he'd let my brother's debt go." As she stumbled over her words, Porter saw red.

"He said that?" The words came out as a growl and he wished he'd toned it down when she flinched. He knew what scum Orlando was but the fact that he'd propositioned someone like Elizabeth stunned him. Her family was wealthy, respected and Elizabeth was complete grace and class. The thought of the other man anywhere near her had Porter clenching his hands into tight fists. His short fingernails dug into his palms, the slight discomfort a welcome distraction.

She nodded, her expression miserable.

"Why didn't you tell *me*?" he pressed insistently. They might not have dated long but he still expected something more from her than this pseudo-stranger routine.

Her face flushed as she shrugged. "I didn't think it would really matter. His *offer* didn't sound like he wanted to kill me or anything. He was just being disgusting."

He frowned. She was right. But Orlando obviously wanted to scare her. Maybe to make her more acquiescent to his 'offer'. Still, opening fire on her in the middle of the day was stupid and amateurish. The man definitely didn't have the business sense his father had.

Porter stared at her and tried to read her expression. Her face was ghostly pale and she simply looked scared. "You're sure there's nothing else you're holding back? It doesn't matter how insignificant."

"I wasn't there very long before you showed up. Everything happened so quickly. And you were at my house last night so you know my brother left before I could talk to him." It happened again. Something like guilt flashed in her eyes. It was lightning fast, but he knew what he'd seen.

He didn't comment on it, but he planned to question her later, when they were away from his brother. She might know something she was too embarrassed to say in front of Harrison. Porter sometimes forgot that Harrison was her boss and it was obvious she was private about her family.

Harrison would probably be annoyed he was cutting this so short, but Porter stood and faced him. "I'm going to get her out of here for now. I'll have one of the teams follow us and get Grant to stop by my place when he gets a break so she can look at those mug shots."

He'd expected Harrison to argue, but his brother simply nodded then motioned with his head toward the hallway. "Let's talk before you guys leave."

"I'll only be a sec," he said to Lizzy.

Nodding, she wrapped her arms around herself in a protective gesture. She might be keeping something from him—and he planned to find out exactly what it was—but no matter what, he planned to keep her under his protection at all costs.

CHAPTER FIVE

"Why aren't we calling the police?" Lizzy asked softly.

Porter glanced at her as he steered away from Harrison's house. That was one of the things his brother had wanted to talk to him about before he left. "Harrison already has. The security team is making a statement about what happened but they're leaving your and Mara's names out of it."

"Why?"

His brother hadn't come out and said it but Porter hadn't needed to ask. "We don't want either of you down at the police station right now." *Where they'd be open targets.* He trusted the cops, especially considering Grant was one, but the idea of dragging both women down to the station when Red Stone Security had more resources than the police department was simply a waste of time. Sure they had a gang squad and theoretically could start looking for suspects, but Elizabeth hadn't actually seen anyone she could identify. The security team was making the report and that's all the cops needed. It's not like the cops could put her in protective custody once she made a statement anyway. Even if they did, Red Stone could still do a better job. They protected dignitaries and government officials all over the world. Security was their business. Not to mention, Porter didn't trust anyone but himself to keep Elizabeth safe.

"So that's not a vague answer or anything." Slight sarcasm laced her words as she shifted against the passenger seat.

"We're going to take care of this situation ourselves." More specifically, *he* was.

She softly snorted. "Situation? Is that what you call someone shooting at us in broad daylight?"

Against his better judgment he reached out and squeezed her leg. Partially to convince himself she was unharmed. When she gave him a startled look he pulled back and had to force his eyes back on the road. Right now she appeared so lost and scared and all he wanted to do was gather her in his arms. "Harrison said you can work from my place if you want, but he wants you to delegate most of your work if possible."

When she let out a soft huff, he bit back a smile. "It's only temporary and you'll still be getting paid."

"I don't like getting a paycheck for work I'm not doing," she muttered.

Another reason he respected her so much. Before he could respond, she continued.

"I'd like to stop by my parents' house on the way to your place. With everything that's happened in the past twenty four hours I want to tell them in person what's going on and I really want to check up on them."

More than anything Porter wanted to take her straight to his place and keep her under lockdown but he understood her need to see her family. "Okay." After radioing the guys in the SUV following them and letting them know the change of plans, they headed to her parents' house.

* * *

Lizzy fidgeted with her hands as she waited for her parents' gate to recede and let them up the driveway. She wasn't necessarily worried about her parents since they had top of the line security and a giant wall surrounding their estate, but she still needed to see them. Even if she dreaded telling them what had happened with Benny. It would give them more ammunition against her brother, but they had a right to know. And she'd never been particularly good at lying to her mother anyway. So while she knew she could keep it a secret for a little while, eventually she'd slip up and it would create more drama from her parents later. Something she'd rather deal with now than in the future.

As they pulled under the stone covered entryway by the front of the palatial house, her chest tightened even more. This was it. Part of her wished she'd let Porter take her straight to his place but she couldn't be a coward.

"Hey. You okay?" Porter reached out and lightly brushed her cheek with his knuckles. The action took her off guard, as did the concern in his eyes. Okay, the concern wasn't really surprising, but she couldn't take how sweet he was being. It only reminded her of how amazing he was. Sure he was dominating and sometimes a little pushy, but when she needed him, he was there for her.

Her throat tight, she nodded and turned away because she didn't trust her voice. No, she wasn't okay, but getting this over with as fast as possible was the best way to go. Like ripping off a band aid. When it was done she'd be going back to Porter's place. The thought of being cooped up alone with him was terrifying on too many levels. Part of her was looking forward to it more than she should, especially considering the circumstances. But the other part, the part that lived in the real world, knew that her emotions were high right now and if anything physical happened between them it would be a mistake they'd both regret.

Moments after she rang the doorbell, the oversized, ornate, custom-made door flew open. Abigail, the older woman who kept order in her parents' house, let out a yelp of delight. "Lizzy! You don't come by here enough." She quickly pulled Lizzy inside and into a tight embrace.

The petite, dark-haired woman Lizzy considered a second mother finally stepped back and looked her up and down with a critical eye. She frowned, like she always did when she saw her. "You're too skinny."

Lizzy bit back a smile at Abigail's standard phrase— she also told her brothers they were too thin when they came by. Turning to Porter, she said, "Porter, this is Abigail. She takes care of everything around here." And she did. When Lizzy and her brothers had been young, Abigail had watched all of them when her parents worked— which had been *very* often. When she wasn't watching them, she was keeping an eye on every other employee in the house. Gardeners, housekeepers, it didn't matter. If they needed something, they went to Abigail first, not her parents. Nothing ever got past her.

After introductions were made, Abigail took Lizzy's arm and led her toward the back of the house, to the lanai no doubt. "It's Wednesday so your parents are still at the country club but they'll be home soon and..."

Lizzy half-listened when she heard Porter's phone ring. He glanced at the caller ID then immediately answered. From the conversation she guessed he was talking to Grant. Though guilt jumped inside her, she realized this would be the perfect time to figure out what her brother's note had meant. Benny had told her to check their secret childhood hiding place and until she knew what he'd hidden there she didn't want to tell anyone else. Even Porter.

"Abigail, would you mind bringing us tea and snacks out on the lanai?" she asked quietly.

"Of course not." Abigail patted her hand and hurried off in the direction of the kitchen.

Once Lizzy and Porter stepped outside, she made a vague motion with her hand that she'd be right back. He frowned at her but didn't stop talking to his brother. After walking the length of the pool, she then rounded the corner of the pool house. Without turning her head she knew she was out of Porter's line of sight. Picking up her pace, she practically sprinted across the yard to the corner where a giant oak tree stood.

In the past decade it had grown larger but the odd shaped knot near the base hadn't changed much. When she and Benny had been kids they'd often hidden notes there for each other. Barely nineteen months apart in age, they'd been much closer with each other than with their other two brothers who were five and six years older.

Reaching through the small slit opening at the center of the knot, she felt around until she grasped a small metal box. Quickly she pulled it out and opened it, not sure what to expect. Her brow furrowed at the gold key inside it but she took it out and shoved the box back where she'd gotten it.

Opening her palm as she stood, she turned the key over. It was gold and smaller than her house key and there was an 'M' engraved on it, but she had no idea what it was for. Benny had said she'd know what to do with whatever she found here, but as she stared at it, she didn't have a clue. Just great. Why did her brother have to be so cryptic?

"Lizzy." Porter's deep voice caused her to freeze for a moment before she spun around to face him.

His pale blue eyes glittered like flecks of ice as he assessed her. "What are you doing?"

"Nothing." Shrugging, she shoved her hands in her pockets. The skirt she wore was slim fitting and she knew once she removed her hands he'd be able to see the outline of something in her left pocket but there wasn't time to hide it anywhere else.

She thought about telling him what she'd found but quickly brushed that idea aside. Porter had already made it clear what he thought of Benny and she wanted to find out what the key opened first. If it posed a danger to her or anyone in her family, she didn't want to be responsible for putting it in the wrong hands.

He stalked toward her with the grace of a jungle animal. Her heart jumped in her throat. Not because she was afraid he'd hurt her, but because of that unmistakable predatory look in his eyes. He used to look at her like that right before kissing her. The distance between them closed in seconds.

Before she could think about backing away, his big hand closed around her waist and held firm. Instinctively she started to tug against him, but he wouldn't let her.

"You are a terrible liar," he murmured before leaning so close his mouth nearly touched her ear.

She tried to suck in a deep breath but found it impossible. Her lungs refused to expand. The spicy scent of his cologne and something that was pure Porter twined around her. It made her think of sex. Hell, everything about him made her think of that. Her breathing was shallow and all she could hear was the sound of her own heartbeat. Like a bass drum it thumped in her ears with no reprieve.

When his hands slid down her hips in a sensuous stroke, she froze. *What was he doing?* Her mind told her to pull back and out of his embrace before they did anything stupid. But it was hard to care about reason when he was holding her so tight, when she could practically feel the sensual energy pulsing from him. She started to place her hands on his shoulders until she realized what he intended. Then it was too late. He'd reached into her pocket and plucked the key out.

His eyes glinted with frustration and a touch of anger. "You want to tell me what this is?"

Rage and embarrassment burned inside her that he'd used her attraction to him against her. She could feel her cheeks flame. She'd been about to throw her arms around him when he'd simply been feeling her up for that key. Despite her heated face, she held his gaze. "Not particularly."

"Then why'd you lie?"

"I—"

"What. Is. This?" Each word was punctuated and precise.

She crossed her arms over her chest. "I don't know, okay?"

"Where did it come from?"

The note her brother had left said not to trust anyone but Porter wasn't just anyone. And he had resources she didn't. "If I tell you, you have to promise you won't tell your brothers...Or your father or anyone at Red Stone." She figured covering all her bases was the smartest thing she could do under the circumstances. Porter was smart and would figure out a loophole if she let him.

He stared hard at her, his eyes turning glacier cold for a moment. She could practically see the wheels turning in his head. He glanced down at the key and turned it over in his hand. His expression was thoughtful. "I'm pretty sure this is a safe deposit box key because I have one just like it. Is this from your brother?"

She didn't respond.

"I'll take that as a yes," he muttered. When she didn't say anything else, he growled at her. "Do you know why Orlando came after you? I can't believe you're holding back information when your best friend could have been hurt today." There was no hiding the disgust in his voice.

She jerked back. His words were like a slap across the face, stinging and brutal. She would have never done anything to endanger Mara or...anyone. "I told you I don't anything about Orlando's motives and I'm not lying!"

"Then what aren't you telling me?" He stared at her as if he didn't quite believe her.

Lizzy rubbed her palms against her skirt. "Benny left me a note the other night. All he said was that he left me something in our childhood hiding place and that I'd know what to do with it. But I *don't*. I have no clue what that key goes to or if it's a safe deposit box key like you said. And if it is, I don't even know what bank it's for."

Porter shoved the key in his pocket. "Do you still have that note?"

Her lips pulled into a thin line as she nodded. "Yeah, it's in my purse."

"Good. I want to see it *now*." There was none of the softer, gentler side of Porter she'd come to know in his voice or his expression. Right now he was angry with her and she wasn't sure that she blamed him. She doubted there was anything in the note he'd be able to decipher that she hadn't, but a twinge of guilt slipped into her veins. Maybe she should have told him about it from the beginning. She shouldn't care what he thought about her but right now she hated the mistrust she saw in his eyes. Aloofness or annoyance she could deal with, but this was a side of Porter she never wanted to see again.

* * *

Orlando slammed the door to his office shut and headed for the balcony of the second story room. Even the perfect sunny view of the Atlantic did nothing to calm his rage.

None of his men could find Benito Martinez. At least part of his plan to scare Elizabeth had gone into effect but with Benny missing he lost a lot of leverage with her. He couldn't threaten to hurt her brother if he wasn't around. Not to mention Benny still owed him money.

Yes, it was a pittance compared to what he was bringing in monthly but in this business he couldn't appear weak. Especially since he'd just taken over for his dead father.

Right now people in the industry were looking at him, judging him, *wanting* him to fail. No doubt expecting that he wouldn't be able to fill his father's shoes. As he blindly stared at the ocean one of his private cell phones rang in his pocket. He didn't give this number out to many people, so even though he didn't recognize it, he answered on the second ring. "Yeah?"

"Hello, Orlando."

Speak of the devil. "Where the hell are you, Benny?"

The other man snorted softly. "Like I'm going to tell you."

"I'm eventually going to find you so make things easy on yourself and—"

"Enough. I'm not paying your money back and you are going to leave my sister alone. *Forever*." Benny sounded sober and sure of himself, a very rare occurrence for this pathetic man.

Orlando gave a sharp bark of laughter as he walked back into his office. "You just keep digging yourself into a deeper hole, *amigo*."

"I'm not your friend and I'm going to tell you exactly why you will leave Elizabeth alone. I have something of yours and unless you want me to release it to the Feds, you'll do what I say."

"*You* have something of mine?" Doubtful. Orlando was ruthless in checking people when they came to his home. No wires, no weapons, and he had scramblers set up all around his house to make it almost impossible for the Feds or the locals to listen in on him. Not that he did much business at his house anyway. But it paid to be careful.

"Why don't you check that false bottom in your desk and tell me?" There was a smug satisfaction in Benny's tone. Also something he'd never heard from the other man before.

For the first time in as long as he could remember, Orlando experienced real fear. As Benny's words registered, something glacial slithered over Orlando's skin, chilling him straight to his bones despite the even temperature in the room. "What did you just say?"

"Check it," Benny ordered.

Orlando's hands actually shook as he did what the other man said. It took a few tries to get the bottom off—the seaming was impossible to see with the naked eye thanks to brilliant craftsmanship.

His hiding spot was *empty*.

A dull ringing started in his ears as if he'd been smashed in the back of the head with a bat. Benny had stolen from him?

His father had always taught him to hide things most treasured in plain sight. Safe deposit boxes were discovered, safes could be broken into and those were often the first places anyone with *any* training looked. So Orlando had kept his most cherished possession close at hand—in case it needed to be destroyed. He'd always felt smug that it was hidden right under everyone's noses.

Now, all smugness was buried and only the rising bile in his throat remained. "You son of a—"

"Save the threats and the curses. I just want to be left alone or I go to the Feds. But not before I make copies of what I took and send it to *everyone* you work with."

Those words almost stopped Orlando's heart. Or at least that's what it felt like. "When did you take it?" He wasn't sure why he asked. That wasn't important. But some morbid part of him needed to know.

"When you invited me over for that fight." Now Benny laughed, the sound sharp and cutting. "I didn't even know if I'd find anything in your office but you have the same ridiculously expensive desk as my dad. Imagine my surprise..." He trailed off again for a moment before continuing. "I thought that was why you brought me to your house yesterday, because you knew what I'd done."

The other man's words hung heavy in the air and heavier in Orlando's heart. Getting Benny to place that large bet on the televised UFC fight had been part of Orlando's ultimate plan to blackmail Elizabeth into aligning herself with him. Of course he'd checked everyone when they'd entered his home but when they'd left...Orlando never would have considered *Benny* enough of a threat to take anything of value from him. Least of all *this*. He'd gotten cocky and stupid in his desire to use the pathetic junkie. "You have signed your own death warrant and that of all those closest to you.

I'll start with that pretty sister of yours. But I'll play with her for a long time before I kill her," he growled.

Benny sucked in a sharp breath. "Anything happens to her and I'll not only do everything I said, I'll post copies of it on the Internet." The phone line went dead.

For a moment, Orlando stared at the phone, disbelieving that Benny had actually hung up on him. *Him.*

With a snarl he heaved his arm back and threw his phone across the room. It splintered into pieces against the wall before falling onto the plush carpet with a soft thud. Orlando's hands balled into fists. He needed to break something. Namely Benny's face.

As he stared at his Louis XV style vintage desk he wanted to rip it apart with his bare hands, one piece at a time. The desk had been his father's. Expensive, sturdy, masculine. He'd kept it out of respect for the man and because it had always made him feel powerful sitting behind the large thing. Now it could burn to ashes for all he cared.

His father had been wrong and now Orlando would pay the price for it. But not if he got to Elizabeth first. No matter what Benny said, Orlando knew the degenerate wouldn't let her die. He'd trade his soul before that happened.

As he managed to calm his erratic breathing he realized that things had drastically changed. He needed Elizabeth now for more than just arm candy and he didn't care about the collateral damage anymore. One way or another he'd find and keep her. In doing so he'd bring Benny to his death and keep all his secrets. If he didn't and what Benny had stolen got out...Orlando was a walking dead man.

CHAPTER SIX

Porter tried to keep his eyes on the road but was finding it increasingly harder to keep his focus off Elizabeth. She wore a form-fitting, strapless dark blue dress that hugged all her curves and showed off miles of sexy tanned legs. Sitting in the passenger seat next to him, her legs were crossed, causing the slit that ran up her thigh to splay open seductively. But he knew she wasn't trying to tease him. She'd been completely distracted from the moment they'd gotten into his SUV. Probably because they'd left the relative safety of his home and she knew she wasn't as guarded anymore.

Even though he didn't doubt his ability to protect her, he'd had a team of guys assigned downstairs to cover the elevator entrance from the parking garage of his condo and two guys standing guard directly outside his front door. Not subtle and definitely not a long-term option but for now it was the only choice they had.

He *had* to keep Elizabeth safe.

And if he had his way they wouldn't have left his condo for anything in the world. Anything *except* his younger brother's engagement party. Porter and Elizabeth were both in the wedding—he as the best man and she as the maid of honor. There would be extra security at the party and it was a very low key affair, not highly publicized, so he wasn't worried about anything happening on site. It was transporting Elizabeth there that had him worried. He didn't like bringing her out in the open.

"Are you worried about tonight?" Her quiet voice echoed through the vehicle's interior and he found her staring intently at him, her brown eyes wide. She wore her emotions so vividly, it pained him to see the worry in her gaze.

Hell yeah. "No. Security will be tight and we're not going to stay that long. Just long enough to make an appearance, do some toasts and then I'm getting you out of there." He'd expected an argument but when she simply nodded he realized how scared she must be.

Not that it was surprising, but after Grant had stopped by so she could look at mug shots—a fruitless exercise—she'd holed up in his guestroom the past couple hours working on her laptop. She'd been so wrapped up in her work he'd had to remind her when it was time to get ready for the party. At her parents' house they'd briefly argued about her keeping her brother's letter a secret from him, but he hadn't had the heart to push her too much. Tomorrow morning they planned to go to Porter's bank to see if it was the right bank for the safe deposit key. The 'M' engraved onto it was a very distinctive symbol for one of the biggest banks in Miami. Since he had a key almost identical to the one Benny had left, it was the best starting point.

If her brother had been smart, he'd have put her name on the account but until they got there they wouldn't know. Whatever was inside that box—if anything—had better redeem Benny or Porter was ready to hurt the guy himself. Well, after Orlando Salas.

With Elizabeth so subdued and not even mustering enough attitude to argue with him—he found he missed her feistiness more than he'd ever admit to her.

"I hate that I've dragged you into this mess," she said quietly.

Frowning, he pulled through the intersection. None of this was her fault. "You didn't do anything—"

The sound of screeching tires alerted him a split second before a Bronco clipped the front of his vehicle, sending them into a tailspin. His neck and shoulders tensed as he gripped the steering wheel for control. "Just perfect," he muttered under his breath as he started to straighten them out.

While he slowed and righted the SUV, sudden sharp bursts of gunfire hailed around them. It sounded like hail crashing down as rounds sprayed the bullet resistant windows. The fist around his heart tightened as reality crashed over him. They were under a full attack.

Elizabeth screamed and ducked down in her seat, sending the contents of her clutch purse scattering everywhere.

"Hang on," he muttered, willing himself to stay calm. If the SUV wasn't armored, he'd be more worried.

Gripping the wheel, he managed to keep moving forward and stay focused on their surroundings. Getting boxed in right now was not an option. Cars and trucks honked from all directions. Even though they had a security team following them he wasn't worried about staying with them. His only priority was getting Elizabeth out of there.

He floored the gas pedal and shot through a red light. Elizabeth was gripping the door handle with one hand and the center console with the other as she crouched lower, but she was otherwise unharmed.

"Can you reach your cell phone?" he asked, his heart in his throat. Elizabeth should never have been placed in a situation like this and he hated the fear he saw on her face.

She bent down to where it had fallen to the floor and grabbed it. "Who do you want me to call?"

"No one. Take out your SIM card and battery."

She looked confused but popped the back of the phone off. He glanced in the rearview mirror again. He doubted anyone had planted a tracking device on his vehicle or even her phone but he didn't have time to check. And he wasn't taking any chances. She'd been at Orlando's house long enough for one of his men to have planted something on her so he'd rather be paranoid than dead.

When she'd done as he asked, he rolled down her window a scant few inches. "Keep the SIM card, throw out everything else."

She hesitated for a millisecond, but did as he asked.

He took an abrupt turn, earning a quick yelp from Elizabeth. At least she wasn't the crying, screaming type. *Thank God.* He couldn't handle that right now and it would just be harder on her if she lost control. So far she seemed to be handling things okay but after the day she'd had, he just hoped she wasn't going into shock.

"Where are we going?" Her quiet voice tugged at his heart, making him want to head to Orlando's and put the guy out of his misery.

"I'll keep you safe. I promise." It was all he could offer. Right now he wasn't sure where he was taking her. Red Stone had a few safe houses located around Miami for emergency situations but he wasn't going to take her to any of them on the chance that Orlando knew about them. It was unlikely, but with Elizabeth's life at stake, there was no room for error.

He steered them down a few side-streets and deeper into the heart of Miami. Bright blue, green and various tropical colored houses flew by them. As he took another turn, his death grip on the steering wheel lessened. There wasn't anyone following them that he could see. Even his security team wasn't visible. One of the guys had tried radioing him but he'd snapped it off. It wasn't far-fetched that one of Orlando's men could be listening in on the right frequency.

Porter slowed and turned down a dead end street. It was lined with old, one-story Florida homes that displayed awnings and jalousie windows. Everything was so damn quiet and peaceful it was hard to believe they'd just been under fire minutes before.

"What are we going to do?" Elizabeth's voice shook.

"We've got to ditch this vehicle," he said as he kicked the SUV into park. It was the best answer he could give her.

She wrapped her arms around herself tightly. "Okay."

More than anything he wanted to lean over and comfort her, promise her everything would be all right—but now wasn't the time. He glanced in his rearview mirror before he bent to grab an extra gun he kept stowed under the driver's seat, but he froze. An SUV—not the Bronco that had clipped them—slowed then parked a few houses back. He twisted around in his seat. A man emerged from a vehicle carrying what looked like—his heart stopped.

Was that a hand rocket?

For a split second, Porter thought he was seeing things. He was in Miami, not a warzone. Without pause, he grabbed the gun then unstrapped Elizabeth's seat belt and grasped her slim arm.

"What are you doing?" she shrieked and struggled against his unforgiving hold.

He knew her instinct to fight was kicking in because he was manhandling her. Instead of answering, he opened his door and forcibly dragged her across the console. Luckily she didn't weigh much. "Run!" he shouted.

As they tumbled on to the sidewalk, he hauled her to her feet and shoved her toward one of the houses. Blood rushed loudly in his ears as he tried to get her to safety. He risked a glance over his shoulder. The guy had the weapon aimed, was about to fire. Porter wrapped his arms around her waist and tackled her to the grassy surface, using his body to protect hers.

A hissing sound streaked through the air then the SUV lifted a few feet off the ground, landing with a sickening boom. A ball of smoke and flames engulfed the vehicle and climbed into the night sky as parts and pieces flew in every direction, landing with loud thuds. The heat licked at his back, but adrenaline coursed through him.

Stay alive. Keep Elizabeth alive.

His thought process was simple.

Pinned beneath him on her back, Elizabeth's dark eyes widened as she gaped at him. He quickly tugged her to her feet. Now she definitely wasn't fighting him. She kicked off her high heels and they ran full force across one of the front yards. Once they rounded the one-story house, Porter jumped the chain link fence into a bordering backyard, then lifted her under her arms and slung her over. Now was no time to be gentle.

They needed to put distance between them and the man who'd just tried to blow them up with a hand rocket. Porter hadn't gotten a good look at it, but it had looked like an AT4 or an RPG. Either way, they were in a very bad situation. Aim didn't have to be exact with a hand rocket. As long as someone could hit in the general vicinity of their target, damage was guaranteed.

This just brought up a whole new mess of questions. Why would Orlando Salas send someone to come after Elizabeth with an RPG in the middle of Miami? Granted, Porter knew Orlando had connections to arms dealers—he did sell drugs after all—but this attack screamed desperation. Porter guessed it had something to do with whatever was in that safe deposit box. Which meant getting to it before anyone else was now paramount.

"We've got to find another car," he said so Elizabeth would know he had some semblance of a plan.

"Yes." She was panting next to him, but she kept up as they ran across the backyard.

Rounding the corner of another one story house, he motioned to Lizzy to keep her back against the wall. She complied without comment.

Hugging the wall, they inched along the side of the house. The fence didn't extend all the way around the yard so once they had visibility of the front yard and part of the neighborhood, Porter pulled out his gun. He hated doing this, but it was the only way to stay alive.

He turned to Elizabeth. "I need you to be my lookout. If you hear or see anything suspicious, run and don't look back. Then find a pay phone and call Harrison or Grant."

She grabbed his arm, fingers curling into his flesh. "What are you going to do?"

"I'm finding us a car."

"Okay." Her voice wobbled, but she crouched down against the corner of the wall.

Keeping his gun low, he stepped out from their hiding place and visually scanned the rest of the neighborhood.

Two houses down, he spotted an old Volkswagen Beetle. Easy to hotwire. He motioned to Lizzy to follow him. Hotwiring was a skill he'd picked up as a teenager. Not something he'd ever been proud of, but now he was damn thankful for the ability. In less than thirty seconds, he'd hotwired the white car and they were heading deeper into the heart of Miami.

* * *

Lizzy's heart pounded wildly in her chest as she sank down onto the closed toilet seat of the cheap motel room Porter had checked them into—after paying with cash. Her legs trembled and she could barely stand as it was. She couldn't believe what had just happened. Terrified didn't even begin to cover what she was feeling.

Someone had blown up Porter's SUV with a freaking rocket launcher or something. And *they* could have been in it when it happened. If it hadn't been for Porter dragging her out of it she'd be dead. Another shudder snaked through her.

Porter was on the phone with Harrison in the adjoining bedroom letting him know they wouldn't be coming to the engagement party tonight so she'd taken the chance to escape for some privacy. No need to let Porter see what a mess she was. This whole situation was her fault. Or, more specifically, her brother's fault. She might want to keep him out of trouble but whatever Benny had gotten himself into was big and really bad. She didn't want to think the worst of him, but other people she cared about had almost been killed because of their involvement with her. First her best friend, and now Porter. Not to mention innocent bystanders.

She attempted to take a deep breath but her lungs felt too small. Her entire body shook and it was taking what little grasp on self-control she had left not to break down into a puddle of tears.

Porter was so efficient and was handling everything so she didn't want to appear weak, especially when this was her mess. *Not his.* If not for her he'd never have gotten dragged into this. Still...hot tears burned her eyes and began to spill over, carving a hot path down her cheeks.

Crap.

She couldn't cry. Not now. If she started, she'd never stop. Her tears, however, didn't listen to her command. To her horror, more pooled in her eyes and they just kept flowing.

A soft knock on the bathroom door jerked her head in that direction.

"Lizzy?" Porter called softly.

He was using her nickname. Just great. She couldn't handle gentleness right now. If he was aloof maybe it would snap her out of this pseudo-breakdown.

"Lizzy?" He said her name again, this time louder and there was no mistaking the concern in that deep voice.

She opened her mouth but only a squeak came out. Mortification welled up inside her. She cleared her throat and tried again. "I'm fine," she rasped out, ignoring how watery and pathetic she sounded.

When he didn't respond she figured he'd give her some space. Leaning forward, she spread her knees and put her head between them. Somehow she had to get control. As she took a deep breath, the bathroom door swung open.

Porter stood in the doorway, his jacket off, his tie loosened and concern on every inch of his face. He swore softly and before she could react he was kneeling in front of her. "Are you all right?"

How could he be so calm? They'd almost been killed. "I'm fine. Sorry you have to see me like this." She batted away some of her tears and for the moment they abated.

Frowning, he cupped her face with one hand and gently wiped her cheek with the pad of his thumb. "You don't have anything to apologize for," he murmured.

The feel of his callused hand on her skin quickly dried the rest of her tears. In a split second her emotions jumped from still-terrified to turned-on and getting hotter. Good Lord, what was wrong with her?

As she blinked away the blurriness her leftover tears caused, the heat in Porter's blue eyes seemed to glow in the small, dimly lit room. "Don't I?" The question came out as a whisper.

He growled something low in his throat. She couldn't understand what he said—if he'd said anything at all.

Still staring at her, he slid his hand back farther until he cupped her head. His grip was dominating but not too tight. Her lips parted as she gazed at him. Anything that happened between them now would likely be a mistake. It was so hard to care though when she craved a release. Anything to take off the edge of the fear crawling around inside her like angry spiders.

Porter was everything she needed and wanted.

Strength.

Stability.

Pure, masculine power.

Lord, the power that emanated from him was enthralling. A shiver rolled over her that had nothing to do with the temperature of the room and everything to do with the man in front of her.

He swallowed once, *hard*, as he stared at her. "You kill all my good intentions." His voice sounded as unsteady as her quaking insides felt.

"Right back at ya," she murmured.

Porter wanted to kiss her. She could see it in his eyes. He was definitely contemplating it but he was also torn. Probably held some honorable thought that right now she was vulnerable and he didn't want to capitalize on it.

That honor was one of the things that had originally drawn her to him. But it didn't change the fact that she would never stop loving her brother and Porter would never understand the bond she and Benny had. It would always lie between them and she couldn't let herself fall for a man when she knew she'd always feel guilty for running to help her brother. It would create resentment for both of them.

Instead of doing the one thing she desperately wanted—throwing her arms around Porter's neck and kissing him until they were both breathless and stripping their clothes off in a mad frenzy—she cleared her throat and averted her gaze from his spell binding one.

The moment she did, Porter dropped his hand.

A sigh of relief she hadn't realized she was holding escaped loud enough for him to hear. Guilt jumped inside her at the almost hurt look he gave her but it was gone so fast she wondered if she'd imagined it.

As he stood, she did too. At least she now had a lid snapped shut on her emotions. Instead of looking in the mirror and seeing what a mess she had to be, she followed him to the other room and perched on the edge of the queen sized bed. "So what's going on?"

"I spoke to Harrison and Grant." Instead of joining her on the bed he paced at the end of it, looking like an animal trapped in a cage. He hated being trapped here, feeling useless. She understood because she felt the same way.

"And?"

"Harrison definitely understands why we won't be at the party tonight but he wants us to go to one of Red Stone's safe houses."

But Porter didn't. He'd already told her as much and she agreed with his reasoning. On the off chance Orlando had somehow found a mole within Red Stone and knew about the locations of their safe houses around the city, Lizzy had no problem hunkering down in a pay-by-the-hour motel. As crappy as the place was, discomfort was an easy trade-off for staying alive. "What about Grant?"

"He's ah…not happy with me. He had already heard about the blown up SUV before I called—didn't know it was one of Red Stone's of course, but it's not every day something like this happens in Miami. He wants to bring us in to make a statement and put us both under protective custody."

Lizzy tensed at his words. If they were in custody she couldn't check out what that key opened up. And more importantly, she couldn't protect her brother. He'd obviously gotten in over his head and she didn't want to be somewhere with no way to help him. "I'm not—"

"We're not going anywhere. The plan is still the same. Tomorrow we go to the bank—hopefully it's even the right one—and see if you have authorization to that safe deposit box. He might not like it, but Grant isn't going to tell anyone we were driving that SUV."

She inwardly sighed in relief. Porter obviously had a different reason for not wanting to go into custody and it had nothing to do with keeping her brother out of trouble. Whatever Porter's reasons were, she didn't care as long as they were both on the same page. "Then what?"

"That depends on what's in the box."

Wasn't that the truth? So much depended on what her brother had left for her. If only she could get hold of him. But of course he'd disappeared again. She stifled a yawn and looked at the bed she sat on.

Despite the grungy motel room the sheets held the faint scent of fresh detergent and there weren't any visible stains on the covers. Not that she really cared at the moment. Her eyes felt as if sandbags weighed on them. There was nothing else they could do tonight and she was starting to crash. It was like she'd been on a rollercoaster and was in an utter freefall. She'd been so high on adrenaline barely an hour before and now all she wanted to do was sleep and block out the rest of the world.

"If you want to take the bed I'll take the chair," Porter said, motioning to where he'd draped his jacket earlier. The cheap wooden chair that sat next to the equally cheap table.

She supposed it was meant to be a breakfast nook of some sort but both pieces of furniture looked as if they might fall apart from a soft breeze. Not to mention he'd already risked so much for her. She wouldn't make him sleep like that. "We're both adults. We can share this bed, but..." She glanced down at her rumpled, torn and dirty dress. While she didn't want to sleep in it, it was better than sleeping in only her panties. Especially when the only thing that would be separating them was a flimsy white sheet.

"You can sleep in my shirt." Porter was already unbuttoning his oxford style shirt and handing it to her before she could think of saying no.

Part of her wanted to protest but the most feminine part of her really wanted to see what was underneath his clothes again. When he bared himself to her, it took a moment to catch her breath. Yep, still as sexy as ever. Her fingers itched to trace along the taut muscles of his chest and trail down the ripped eight pack of his abdomen. And she would follow with her mouth. Slowly.

When Porter cleared his throat, her head snapped up and she realized she'd been blatantly staring. Her face flamed as he gave her a knowing, almost satisfied look. Brushing aside her embarrassment, she stood and grabbed the shirt from him. "Thanks," she murmured.

It was definitely going to be a long night. Tired or not, the thought of sharing a bed with Porter made her knees go weak and the already growing heat between her legs increase to scorching hot levels.

After buttoning up his shirt—which smelled deliciously like Porter, all spicy male goodness—she exited the room to find Porter already lying in the bed. He'd turned off the lamp on the nightstand so the neon lights from the sign outside shined through the thin white curtain, providing their only illumination. The cover was pulled down and only the sheet covered Porter's lower half. When she spotted his pants on the chair on top of his jacket she wondered if he was wearing boxers or anything beneath that sheet. It was dark so it was too hard to tell.

Unfortunately her imagination ran rampant. Mentally shaking herself, she hurried to the bed and slid under the sheet, careful to avert her gaze from checking him out too much.

Turning on her side and away from him, she stared at the outline of the flickering neon light. Several moments passed and while his breathing was steady, she knew he wasn't sleeping. Despite her adrenaline crash, the need to talk to him was overwhelming. "So...was hotwiring cars a skill you learned in the Marines?" She knew he'd been in for eight years before going to college then working for his father. But the hotwiring thing was something he'd never told her about.

He chuckled softly behind her. "Definitely not. Though that skill came in handy once or twice overseas when I needed to get out of a tight spot."

The sheet rustled beneath her as she turned over to face him. "I know how long you were in, but how much time did you actually spend overseas?"

As he shifted a little and turned fully in her direction, it was hard to see more than the outline of his face with the light behind her. "Almost seven years."

Her eyebrows raised. "That's like ninety percent of your military career. Was it all...in a warzone?"

He nodded. "For the most part, yes. I spent about six months in Africa though. Not fun, but not a warzone."

Lizzy paused for a moment. "I didn't even know we had a base there...Do you mind me asking you these questions?"

Porter shook his head, making a quiet swishing sound against his pillow. "No, and if you're interested, the base is in Djibouti, in the Horn of Africa."

"Oh. Why don't you mind me asking? When we were, uh, together, I kind of got the impression that your military career was off limits."

He was silent for a long moment, but he eventually spoke. "I normally don't like talking about it with anyone. It had nothing to do with you personally. After what you've been through today, I figure you can ask any damn thing you want. You reacted better under first-time gunfire than some trained men I've seen."

Lizzy's eyebrows drew together. "Really? I still feel like a mess, like I can't get a grip on the shakiness inside me...I'm afraid that feeling won't ever go away."

Wordlessly he scooted a few inches closer and wrapped an arm around her waist and tugged her toward him. She didn't even think about resisting. She laid her head on his chest and listened to the steady beat of his heart. She hadn't even realized how much she'd needed to be held until that moment, but his arms were like solid anchors. "Thank you," she whispered against his bare skin.

In response he squeezed her a fraction closer and kissed the top of her head. "Get some sleep, Lizzy," he whispered.

Lizzy. She loved when he called her that. Sighing, she snuggled closer. His heartbeat was so soothing and just like that, calmness threaded through her and she listened to what her body desperately needed. Sleep.

CHAPTER SEVEN

Porter tried to move without jostling Elizabeth but found he liked the way her lithe body draped against his a little too much. Last night it had been impossible not to hold her close to him. Not when she'd so obviously needed that extra contact.

About an hour ago she'd shifted in her sleep and was now wrapped around him and holding on tight. As if he was her pillow and she couldn't bear to let him go. One of her slim legs was thrown over his lower body and all he had as a barrier was boxers. Now he was rethinking his decision to sleep in only them.

In all the fantasies he'd imagined of Elizabeth in bed with him, none of them had included this much clothing or a hard-on he couldn't do anything about. When she rubbed a hand down his chest and burrowed her head deeper against his neck he let out a soft groan, unable to hold it back.

At the sound, Elizabeth stirred and slowly looked up at him. Her espresso-colored eyes were confused. Frowning, she blinked a couple times then looked down at their entwined bodies. The shirt of his she'd worn had pushed up to the enticing curve of her hip and with the sheet thrown off them, a lot of her skin and very skimpy underwear was showing. He could see the soft curve of her butt and it was taking all his restraint to not trace his hand down her back and keep going until he'd cupped her even tighter against him.

His own reaction was obvious and she had to feel it on her inner thigh considering her leg was slung seductively across his body. When she looked back at him, her cheeks flushed pink but she didn't make a move to get off him.

Instead, she licked her lips. Slowly. *Nervously.* She almost appeared half asleep but it was the fire and heat in her eyes that pushed him over the edge. That wasn't sleep, it was lust.

He was a goner.

Uncaring about the consequences, he tangled his fingers in her dark hair and brought her mouth to meet his. Her tongue met his stroke for stroke. Feeling almost frenzied, he flipped her over so that he was on top of her. He couldn't stop kissing her. Couldn't stop the hunger raging through him.

After opening up to her last night, even as short as that conversation had been, he wanted to take from her. Take and give her so much pleasure she couldn't see straight. To lose himself in her sweet body. Ever since their breakup he'd been fighting his damn feelings for her and he was tired of it. Tired of trying to pretend she hadn't gotten under his skin in the worst way.

She didn't attempt to stop what they were doing. No, she completely molded against him. Elizabeth spread her thighs wider to accommodate him as he settled between her legs. What he wouldn't give to strip away the few barriers of clothing between them and sink deep inside her.

This had disaster written all over it. Her emotions had to be high and after two near-death experiences yesterday she might not be thinking straight. Might even regret this later. With her writhing underneath his body, so willing, so pliant in his arms, the voice of reason in his head was silenced.

She spread her hands across his chest, slightly digging her nails into him when she reached his shoulders. The feel of her touching even that expanse of skin made him ache. He could only imagine what it would feel like to have her hand grasped around his erection. Holding him. Stroking him.

With that thought, his hips jerked against hers and she moaned into his mouth.

Reaching between them he blindly tugged at the buttons on her shirt. Well, his shirt. Seeing her wearing his clothes had done something primal to him last night. She looked sexier in that than any lingerie. And now his scent would be on her. Soon, in more ways than one.

How he wanted to slide his cock into her over and over until she was crying out his name.

He pulled the flaps of the shirt back and sucked in a quick breath as he got his first view of her naked body. The woman was absolutely perfect. Just like he'd known she'd be. Small breasts, perfect brown nipples—he'd wondered so many damn times what color they'd be— and soft, kissable skin he wanted to rake his teeth and tongue over.

Her fingers tightened on his shoulders and he realized he'd been staring too long. Without pause, he dipped his head and sucked one of her nipples into his mouth. Using his teeth, he lightly tugged until the nub was rock hard and she was quietly moaning underneath him.

"More," she whispered.

Gladly. Smiling, he began lightly circling the taut bud with his tongue and enjoying the way she moved under him with each stroke. He'd barely stimulated her but she was so reactive.

As he kissed his way toward her other breast, a litany of shouts from the next room made them both pause. A woman was shouting obscenities at someone. A man, if the return shouts were any indication. He could ignore them if Elizabeth could. Right now the voice of reason in the back of his head was telling him to put the brakes on. To stop this before things went too far and he fell for her even worse than he already had. Nothing about their relationship had changed between last night and this morning. Keeping his gaze on her bared breasts, he tried to pull back. To listen to that voice in his head.

When she slid her fingers through his hair and tugged him toward her breast, he lost the battle.

Dipping down again, he slowly ran his tongue around her areola. As he did, he tweaked her other nipple with his forefinger and thumb, gently rolling and teasing it.

Breathing hard, she wrapped her legs around his waist and began slowly grinding against his erection as he played her body.

"Porter," she breathed out his name so reverently it was like a punch to his system. Her fingers clutched his shoulders and tightened with each stroke of his tongue. "That's perfect." The words were more moan than anything.

He hadn't even gotten started. Reaching between them, he started to cup her mound when his cell phone rang. His hand froze by her lower abdomen and her entire body tensed.

He wanted to ignore it. Ignore everything and keep pleasuring Elizabeth. As he flicked his tongue over her nipple, she shuddered.

Then his phone rang again.

Beneath him Lizzy sighed and loosened her legs from around him, letting them fall completely away from his hips. "It might be one of your brothers," she muttered, looking just as disappointed as he felt.

Clenching his jaw, he leaned over and grabbed his cell off the dresser. Sure enough, it was Grant.

The cursing next door had simmered down to mere shouting, but after these interruptions he knew the moment between him and Elizabeth was over. It was probably for the best. Unfortunately it was hard to think with all her exposed skin. When she started to button her shirt and sit up, he sighed and flipped his phone open.

"Yeah," he practically growled.

"Have you seen the news this morning?" Grant's voice was grim.

Porter's heart beat a staccato rhythm. *What could have happened now?* "No."

A heavy sigh. "That 'little' explosion made the morning news."

"Do the detectives on the case know any details?"

His brother cursed under his breath. "They know the SUV is registered to Red Stone but other than that, they're in the dark."

Porter rubbed a hand over his face. "I don't want you taking any heat for this later. Tell them I was driving it and—"

"Not yet. Right now they're not so much concerned on who was driving it as who *fired* that RPG. I've let one of the detectives know—off the record—to look at the Seventy Ninth Street Gang as a starting point. They're not wasting man hours and they know more than they would have without my help. I still think you two should come in. After what happened it's understandable that you went into hiding but—"

"Forget it."

"Why are you being such a hardass? I know you want to protect Lizzy, but—"

"It's better you don't know everything, Grant." Porter wasn't about to tell his brother about the key they'd found. Not yet. First he wanted to see what was inside the safe deposit box. Not to mention he'd stolen a car the night before. Telling his *detective* brother about that would put Grant in a compromising position and Porter didn't want to put pressure on Grant. Keeping his family uninvolved in all of this was one of his main priorities. Right after keeping Lizzy—no, *Elizabeth*—safe. He forced himself to think of her as Elizabeth. It was the only way to keep his distance from her. Lizzy was the woman he'd dated. The woman he fantasized about. The woman who he'd just been half-naked with. "I'll call you later." Before his brother could protest, Porter ended the call.

When he turned toward the bathroom door he realized Elizabeth had hung his shirt on the knob. Inside the other room he could hear water running. "I'm going to grab some breakfast bars for us," he called through the door as he slipped his shirt on.

"Okay. I'll be out in a sec." Her voice was slightly muffled with the barrier between them.

After checking out the window to make sure there wasn't anyone waiting to ambush him, he opened the door and he headed down the cracked sidewalk toward the main office. He'd seen two snack machines the night before and while there wasn't much inside either one, he knew Elizabeth would be hungry. As soon as they left the motel he planned to find an inexpensive outlet store and buy them both a change of clothes with cash. Since Orlando wasn't as powerful as his father, Alberto, had been, Porter doubted Orlando had the ability to track their credit cards, but at this point he and Elizabeth were staying off all radars.

If they went to the bank wearing their clothes from last night they'd stand out. And Porter had no idea how many spies Orlando had around Miami. Blending in was one of the most important things they could do right now.

After purchasing four snack bars, he walked back to the room. As he strode down the sidewalk he noticed a blue, two-door muscle car cruising through the parking lot at a very slow speed. *Too slow.* It was about eight in the morning but there wasn't any other movement outside the rooms or in the parking lot. When he spotted the blue and black bandanas the two men in the front seat wore around their heads, his heart rate increased. Seventy Ninth Street Gang colors.

Instead of showing a reaction, he peeled open one of the bars and started eating it like he didn't have a care in the world. Keeping his pace normal even though every instinct in his body screamed at him to run, he remained steady until he entered the motel room. If these guys were after Elizabeth they wouldn't want to do anything out in the open. They'd try to strike inside the motel room. Which gave Porter a few moments to get her to safety.

The second he shut and locked the door behind him, he tossed the food and grabbed the extra gun he'd left for Elizabeth on the nightstand.

At that moment Elizabeth walked out of the bathroom wearing her rumpled dress from the night before. She must have read the expression on his face because hers instantly tightened in alarm. "What's going on?"

"I saw what looked like a couple of Seventy Ninth Street Gang members drive by. Could be nothing but we can't leave out the front door." Without waiting for a response, he motioned for her to follow as he headed into the bathroom. In seconds he managed to shove open the small window. He glanced over his shoulder. "We'll crawl out here."

"Okay." With wide eyes, she nodded. After yesterday she was unfortunately aware of just how bad their situation really was, which was probably why she didn't question him.

CHAPTER EIGHT

Lizzy wiped damp palms against her ruined dress. When would this nightmare end? It was as if there was *nowhere* they'd be safe. Not until she and Porter figured out what that blasted key opened up.

After peering out the window, Porter grabbed her by the waist and helped hoist her up through it. Without shoes, the gravelly pavement dug into her bare feet, but it was a small price to pay.

As Porter slid through after her, she heard the distinctive sound of their front door slamming open.

Then male voices.

Her pulse skyrocketed.

"Run," Porter said, his voice barely above a whisper.

With a racing heart, she did just that. Ignoring the biting pain in her feet, she took off with Porter next to her across the parking lot behind the motel.

There was only one car and a green Dumpster in the back and it didn't provide them much cover. She knew Porter had a couple guns on him but without any place to hide and at least two men after them, she was still terrified.

"What are we doing?" she rasped out.

Before he answered, someone shouted loudly behind them. "Hey!"

She risked a quick glance over her shoulder to see a man looking through the window and brandishing a handgun. She almost tripped, but Porter grasped her upper arm, keeping her upright.

"Keep running." His voice was as rock steady as his stride.

How the man could stay so calm right now was beyond her. If she stopped and thought about everything that had happened the past couple days, she was afraid she'd have a breakdown. But not Porter.

The man was like ice.

"See that fence?" He motioned toward their right.

A dilapidated metal fence with multiple wide gaps surrounded a large expanse of patchy grass and pavement. A few rusting basketball hoops and picnic benches were all that remained of what she guessed had once been a play area. "Yeah."

"We're going to cut through there and head to those buildings."

Behind the rundown area stood a plethora of abandoned boarded up warehouses. Her heart jumped into her throat. Considering the less than stellar area of town they were in, she couldn't ignore the thread of fear that slid down her spine. They might be running into something worse than what they were running from.

Before she could voice her fear, a loud engine roared behind them. As they ducked through an opening in the fence she glanced behind them again, unable to stop herself. It was as if a fire breathing monster was at her back—a monster with guns—and she needed to see how far away the danger was.

A two-door car was rumbling around the corner of the motel. She and Porter had enough distance between them that they could make it to one of the warehouses first. The car couldn't cut through the decaying park. Instead it would have to drive all the way around and cut back to reach the warehouses. That didn't lessen her anxiety because if those guys caught up to them...Lizzy shivered.

"Focus on getting to safety." Porter glanced at her as they ran and the determined look on his face gave her the strength she needed.

She sprinted along the paved areas, afraid of what might be in the grass. Needles, broken glass, and only God knew what. At least now she could see what she was running over even if her feet burned with the agony of slamming against the pavement over and over.

Stay alive! The two words screamed in her head. She could deal with any pain if it meant getting away from gun-toting gang members.

When they reached the other side of the park, Porter lifted part of the fallen fence back for her to squeeze through, then followed after. This time she made herself keep her eyes straight ahead. She didn't need to see if the car had rounded the block.

"Almost there," Porter murmured. Grasping her upper arm, Porter guided her toward a three-story building with windows spray painted black or covered with rotting boards.

Her lungs burned but she forced herself to push on. Somewhere behind them she could hear the sound of that car engine getting closer.

The moment they stepped inside the building, Porter scooped her up in his arms.

"What are you doing?"

"Your feet are bleeding. We can't leave a trail." As he spoke he didn't look at her, just glanced around the open expanse of the warehouse. Looking for a place to hide.

He began running across the hard surface toward a stack of decaying wooden crates. Considering he was carrying her, his fast, measured movements were impressive. Moments later he set her down and they hunkered behind the crates.

When he took off his jacket, she frowned. "What are you doing?"

He ripped the arm sleeves off and gently took one of her feet in his hands. "I'd give you my shoes but you'd only trip all over yourself and carrying you isn't a long term option. As soon as we get out of here, I promise to take care of your feet," he whispered. Gingerly, he began wrapping one of her soles with the torn sleeve. His gentleness had the potential to undo her.

The moment the cloth made contact with her exposed skin, the pain hit. Her feet were raw and bloody and now that they'd slowed down, a splintering ache ran up her legs, making all her nerve endings tingle in awful awareness.

The sound of car doors slamming in the distance made her want to scream in frustration. But she held it back as Porter secured the ripped cloth around her other foot.

Using his hands, he motioned behind them to a door with a burned out EXIT sign above it. Understanding, she nodded and followed.

It felt as if tiny knives dug into her soles with each quiet step she made.

"Find the woman!" An accented male voice reverberated off the interior of the warehouse. "Kill the man if necessary, but keep her alive."

Her eyes widened at the vicious orders, but Porter didn't even falter in front of her. Footsteps echoed behind them but they quickly continued onward. They had limited cover right now and unless they got outside soon they'd be discovered.

As they reached the exit door with the blacked out window, Porter slowed, then eased it open a fraction. It slightly squeaked, the sound overly pronounced to her. Glancing through the small opening, Porter nodded that it was clear outside before they slipped through.

Blood rushed loudly in her ears as he gingerly shut the door behind them. Before she could ask what their next move was, he pointed to the right. Two similar looking buildings stood next to the one they'd come out of and the back alley led directly to a street.

The sounds of cars and city life seemed so far away but she knew if they could just get to some semblance of civilization they'd be able to blend in better. Or at least find a place to hide.

As they ran down the back alley toward the street, Porter pulled out his cell phone and dialed someone. "Grant, I need your help. *Now.*"

Despite the pounding in her chest and the bitter taste of fear coating her mouth, she allowed herself a small breath of relief. Help was on the way.

CHAPTER NINE

Orlando tightened his hand around his phone but refrained from slamming it to the pavement by his pool. Instead he shoved it into his pocket then flexed his fingers.

"What did they say?" Miguel asked, referring to Juan and Eddie Ortega, the two brothers of the Seventy Ninth Street gang he'd hired to do his dirty work.

Orlando turned at the sound of his cousin's voice, anger a live thing inside him. One of the bimbos who frequented his house strolled up with Miguel, a glass of champagne in her hand. Orlando knocked it out of her hands. "Get the hell out of here!"

With wide eyes she scampered away, leaving Miguel shaking his head. "Damn, cousin, you've got to stop scaring the girls."

"Fuck them," Orlando snarled. "And fuck Juan and Eddie. They can't do anything right." He'd hired them because they didn't have direct ties to his organization. And they were fairly cheap labor. He should have used his own guys for this operation. Better yet, he should have handled it himself. But he'd gotten a tip from a local junkie this morning who said he'd seen Elizabeth and

Porter at some roach motel and it had been close to the Ortega's neighborhood.

Orlando had put word out on the street to be on the lookout for Elizabeth and sure enough, a tip had eventually come through. Some people would do anything for money, especially drug addicts.

"You see the news?" Miguel asked quietly.

Orlando gritted his teeth. Yet another disaster. Using an RPG in the middle of Miami? It drew way too much attention and could have killed Elizabeth, screwing up his entire plan. "I don't know what they were thinking," he muttered.

His cousin shrugged. "They got overzealous. Wanted to impress you."

Miguel's casual attitude annoyed him, but he bit back a response. Right now he needed his cousin to have his back. Needed someone he could trust on the streets. Especially with Benny still out there. "Have you heard anything about Benny?"

Miguel nodded. "That's what I wanted to tell you. Got a tip that he's shacked up with one of his exes. Another junkie who apparently went straight. Heard someone saw him around her place."

Finally luck was shining down on him. Orlando nodded at two of his guards hovering by the Olympic sized pool a few feet away. "You two come with us."

Miguel fell in stride with him as they headed toward the house. "You don't want to send someone?"

"Not this time." He wanted Benny and he was through depending on anyone else to clean up this mess.

* * *

Porter knelt in front of Elizabeth, careful as he removed the strips of bloodied cloth from her feet. She sucked in a hiss of breath once but other than that, didn't make a sound as he took them completely off.

She sat on the closed toilet lid in the bathroom of a local diner that was open twenty-four hours. Unfortunately it wasn't far from the motel they'd run from, but while they waited for his brother it was the best place to hide and inspect Elizabeth's wounds. The tired looking waitress hadn't glanced twice at them when they'd told her they'd need a minute before ordering. She'd just grunted and nodded as they'd hurried to the restroom in the back of the one-story building. Other than her, there hadn't been anyone else out front.

"You don't have to do that." Elizabeth laid a gentle hand on his shoulder.

Looking up at her in that rumpled dress, a bad case of bed head and dark circles under her eyes, he just wanted to pull her into his arms and get her the hell out of there. "Yeah I do," he murmured, looking back down.

Her feet weren't as bad as he'd originally thought. They were raw but once he got some proper bandages and some serious antibiotics on them, she should be fine. He grabbed a bunch of paper towels and placed them in front of the white sink. There wasn't a mirror in the place, though that was probably a good thing. Neither of them needed to see what they looked like.

"Can you stand?" he asked.

Laughing under her breath, she nodded. "I'm not going to break, Porter. My feet hurt, but this isn't that bad."

As she stood, placing her feet on the paper towels, he put his arm under her shoulders. "Put one foot in the sink."

After washing the blood away, she repeated the process with the other foot then stepped onto fresh paper towels. As he helped her to sit back down, his phone buzzed once in his pocket. When he saw his brother's text, telling Porter that he was outside waiting for them, relief flooded sharp and potent inside him. "Grant's outside," he told Elizabeth.

"Thank God," she muttered as she stood.

After throwing away the bloody towels, Porter peered outside to find the small hallway by the restrooms empty. Thankfully the rest of the diner was the same except for the waitress from earlier. Even though she let out a yelp, Porter picked Elizabeth up and carried her out. "I don't want you walking barefoot on this floor," he murmured as they hurried through the quiet diner.

"I'm not complaining." She tightened her grip around his shoulder.

He turned to the side and pushed open the glass door with his hip. The second they stepped outside, Grant jumped out of the front seat of his four-door police-issued sedan.

Even though he had on sunglasses, Porter could see the tenseness in his brother's shoulders as he approached them. "Shit, you didn't tell me she was hurt."

"*She* is right here and I'm fine. I just need some bandages," Elizabeth said as she shifted against him.

Instinctively Porter glanced around the parking lot, gauging possible threats as he took her to the back seat of Grant's car. When he didn't see anyone, he helped her inside then slid in after her.

Grant immediately got in the driver's seat. Before Porter could ask if his brother had brought what he'd asked, Grant handed him a plastic shopping bag and a small first aid kit.

"I didn't know your size, Lizzy so I guessed." Grant didn't glance at them as he steered out of the parking lot.

"Put on these new clothes first then I'll bandage your feet," Porter said to her when she looked questioningly at the bag Grant had handed them.

"Keep your eyes on the road, Grant," she muttered as she started pulling clothing out.

His brother grunted a non-response as he zoomed down the road and away from the diner.

Despite the situation, Porter grinned as she hurriedly stripped out of the dress and into the fitted pair of dark jeans and tight black T-shirt. He should have given her a little privacy, but he couldn't help and sneak a few glances in her direction. After seeing her half naked this morning he was kicking himself for showing so much damn restraint back when they'd been dating. Since she didn't have a bra Porter could see the outline of her nipples. She cleared her throat and he realized he'd been staring when he caught her gaze.

Her pretty lips pulled together in a thin line. "Do you mind?" she whispered.

Knowing that flirting with her would get him burned he kept his mouth shut, but still couldn't keep from grinning. "Sorry," he whispered back.

She shook her head, but he was relieved to see a small smile tug at her lips. "No you're not."

He shrugged and patted his leg. "Put your foot up here."

Using a small bottle from the first aid kit, he poured hydrogen peroxide on her feet. She hissed but didn't struggle.

As he continued with the ointment and bandages, Grant finally spoke. "What the hell is going on with you two? And don't give me some bullshit story. After the drive-by, the explosion and now some gang members attacking you, why the hell aren't you going into protective custody?"

Porter already hated involving his brother this much. "I already told you—"

"I know what you told me and I also know *you*. Do not fucking lie to me anymore," Grant growled.

Porter met his angry gaze in the rearview mirror, but before he could speak, Elizabeth beat him to it.

"It's my fault." Her voice was quiet, but strong and he realized she was going to tell Grant the truth so he didn't try to stop her. "Benny left me a key. Porter thinks it's to a safe deposit box and I agree with him." She shot Porter a quick look, then returned her gaze to the front seat. "We need to see what's inside it since it's obviously tied to why Orlando wants me dead."

"Captured," Porter corrected quietly.

"What?" Frowning, she turned to look at him.

"That gang member said they needed to take you alive. Which means Orlando wants to use you as a bargaining chip against Benny. Possibly for whatever's in that safe deposit box." Porter looked at his brother again. "We need to get whatever's in that box first and I don't need you involved. You're a cop and if it's illegal you'll have an ethical duty to report it."

Grant was silent for a long moment, then finally gave a short nod. "I don't like it, but you're right. And I'm still following you to whatever bank you're going to. If any of Orlando's guys get a bead on your location, I want to be nearby, especially since you can't bring a weapon inside."

Porter nodded. "Fine with me. Lizzy?" He couldn't help but call her by the nickname as he looked at her.

"What if the contents of the box are illegal?" she murmured even though Grant could hear her.

Porter didn't even want to go there because he knew he'd break a lot of laws to keep her damn brother out of trouble. Not for Benny, but for Lizzy. That scared the shit out of him. But he couldn't say that in front of Grant. "We'll deal with that once we open it, okay?"

Expression grim, she nodded. "Okay. I...I trust you."

It almost seemed to pain her to say the words, but it touched him she'd even opened up to Grant. By telling his brother what was going on it was obvious she trusted his family to some extent.

The longer Porter was around her, the more he realized that walking away from her after this bullshit with her brother and Orlando Salas was over, was going to be damn near impossible.

CHAPTER TEN

Lizzy clasped her hands tightly together in her lap as she stared at the bank looming across the street from her and Porter. The simple building with palm trees and an American flag outside it shouldn't be intimidating.

"You have nothing to be nervous about. As soon as Grant lets us know the bank is clear, you're good to go inside." Next to her in the driver's seat of the car Grant had retrieved for them, Porter was once again the epitome of calmness. He didn't need to say a damn word. The man just made her feel safe simply by being here. After seeing him in action more than once, she knew there was no one she'd rather be with right now than him.

She was thankful for that. For so many years she'd been cleaning up Benny's messes on her own. On an intellectual level she knew she was only enabling her brother. But she didn't know how to *stop* helping him. Turning her back on him seemed cruel when she was the only family member who would have anything to do with him. Having Porter helping her even when she knew what he thought about her brother was a huge relief. She hadn't even realized how stressful taking care of Benny had become until now, when she had someone sharing the burden. "I know. It's just not knowing if this is even the right bank. What if it's not?"

Porter shrugged, those broad shoulders lifting casually. "Then we keep hunting until we find the right one. But...this is one of the most secure banks in Miami and the key looks almost exactly like mine. Your brother might be a junkie but he doesn't strike me as stupid. This is the place he'd hide something important."

Her first instinct was to defend Benny at Porter's use of the word junkie, but he'd almost said the words absently as he intently scanned the area around them for possible threats. He wasn't insulting her brother, just stating a fact. Benny *was* a junkie. Even if he had been clean for a little while, he had an addiction problem. If it wasn't drugs, it was gambling. She needed to come to terms with it and stop making excuses.

Lizzy looked out her tinted window again. The row of tall, skinny palm trees in front of the two story bank swayed in the gentle breeze across the street. And the steady stream of people who had been milling in and out of the international bank only half an hour before had thinned to an almost nonexistent trickle. After another few minutes passed, only one man in a suit stood under the stone overhang outside the building talking on his cell phone. "Can I use your phone again? I want to check my voicemail." Porter's cell was encrypted so she had no worries of them being traced if she used it. Since she'd thrown hers out, she'd been trying to check her voicemail as much as possible on the chance Benny called with more information.

Porter nodded as he pulled it out of his pants pocket and handed it to her. Now that they were both wearing regular clothes and she'd had a chance to brush her hair—and thank God brush her teeth—she felt more like her old self again. Not completely, but anything was better than running around in that dress with no shoes on. The sneakers Grant had brought for her were a little big, but they were cushioned and helped with her soreness.

She quickly dialed her number then punched in the voicemail code. After deleting a message from her mother, and her oldest brother Santos, the bottom of her stomach fell out when she heard Orlando Salas's unmistakably cruel voice on the other end. *"I have something you want and you have something I want. Let's make a trade. If not, the thing you want will disappear. Forever. Call me to make arrangements. And if you tell your fucking bodyguard about this...well, people disappear all the time."* He left a number which she immediately memorized.

She could feel the color from her face drain as the call ended so she slightly turned away from Porter, hoping he wouldn't notice. She wasn't ready to tell him about this call just yet. Especially since Orlando had not-so-subtly threatened him too. Instead of deleting or saving it, she replayed it again. Her hand tightened around the phone, her palm slick with perspiration. She could only assume the 'thing' she wanted was Benny. Orlando had been very careful to leave a fairly generic message. Sure the last bit was threatening, but it was nothing that could get him in trouble with the law. Sneaky bastard. Once she'd heard the number again and was sure she'd committed it to memory, she snapped Porter's phone shut and handed it to him.

"You okay?" he asked, concern in his deep voice and in every line of that handsome face. The man didn't miss a thing. Those eyes of his were so damn searching, so...full of warmth it nearly undid her.

Instead of answering she asked what had been on her mind the past twenty-four hours. "Why are you helping me, Porter? You don't owe me anything. You could have turned me over to your brother and let the cops deal with all this. After today I wouldn't blame you if you did just that."

Something flashed in his eyes, something predatory and primal. It was gone so fast but she knew she hadn't imagined it. "I can't *not* help you, Lizzy. I'd do any damn thing you asked me to." He ground the words out, as if admitting it was painful.

For the second time in minutes, her stomach dropped. Because of what he'd said and his use of her nickname. His voice always softened when he called her Lizzy and she liked it a little too much. "What—"

The buzz of Porter's phone made Lizzy jump. They both looked at it in his palm. "It's Grant," he said as he snapped it open. "Yeah?"

A few 'yeahs' later, he shut the phone once again and looked at her. That heat was still simmering in his gaze. "You're good to go. Grant's inside the lobby." Turning around, Porter grabbed a ball cap from the backseat and handed it to her. "Not super spy material as far as disguises go, but tuck your hair into this and keep your head down. I'm right here, watching you the whole time. We have no idea how many eyes Orlando has on the street. It's better if we're not seen together right now."

She nodded. They'd already gone over this a few times in the past couple hours. Porter had wanted to wait until after the lunch rush to check out the safe deposit box so they'd had time to kill. Having him reassure her that he had her back eased her fear. "Porter..." She didn't know how to put any of her feelings into words. Not when he'd been so amazing. Pushy and bossy sometimes? Definitely.

But the man had stood by her when he had no reason to. They weren't in a relationship and she'd broken up with him. Yet here he was, watching her back. For that alone she wanted to tell him about the message from

Orlando but she couldn't find the words. Orlando had threatened Porter and she couldn't bear the thought of him getting hurt. And what if Porter told his brother about it? Then the cops would get involved and might get her brother killed...No, she needed to see exactly what was in the box first before she made any big decisions.

Guilt swamped through her at not telling Porter but she shoved it back down. Leaning forward, she took his face in her hands and full on kissed him. Tangling her tongue with his, she took a few precious seconds to savor the spicy taste of him. Porter seemed caught off guard for all of a millisecond, but he didn't hold anything back in the kiss. It was raw, hungry and she felt his sensuous strokes all the way to her toes. Heat built inside her, sweeping through her like a tidal wave until she had to force herself to pull back.

Breathing hard, she stared at him for a long moment. She could do this. With Porter outside watching, it would be a piece of cake. A little voice in her head told her to tell him about the phone message from Orlando but there was nothing they could do about it now anyway. Not until she knew what was in that stupid safe deposit box. Better to find out the contents first.

After slipping the plain blue ball cap on her head and grabbing the small backpack Grant had also retrieved for them, she headed across the street.

Once inside she saw Grant lounging in the sitting area. Four short, modular couches were angled together to create a square around a perfectly square glass table. Managing to keep her gaze away from him—even though she was very grateful for his presence—she headed straight for the first open teller.

Though her heart beat like crazy the entire time, once she showed the teller her ID and the gold key, the woman dressed in the sharp black skirt-suit led her down a set of stairs, a long tiled hallway and through two sets of locked doors. Opening the box was a simple thing and once the teller had inserted her matching key and pulled the box out of the slot, the woman left.

The moment the door shut behind her and Lizzy was alone in the cold room with rows and rows of safe deposit boxes, she opened the one on the small wooden table in front of her.

Inside was a thin, long rectangular black notebook. There was nothing else there. Frowning, she flipped it open. As she scanned the pages she realized what she was seeing and for a moment it felt as if her heart actually skipped a beat.

Dates, meeting places, names of some very powerful government officials and what she assumed were bank account numbers were listed all the way back about seventeen years. This must have originally belonged to Alberto Salas, but looking at the current dates she realized

Orlando had held on to it and continued adding information about all sorts of interesting stuff.

The high profile political names were interesting, but also interesting were the listings of some men Lizzy thought were Orlando's competitors. She couldn't be sure, but she'd seen some of the names on the international news enough to know that they were bad men. Drug dealers, arms dealers...bad, bad stuff. And he had information on who they were sleeping with, where they golfed, who they golfed with, how many mistresses they had, who would possibly take a bribe in their organization, who *was* taking bribes. A lot of it just looked like scribbling and random notes. In the right—or wrong—hands, this book could be very powerful. After shoving the notebook into her backpack she pressed the call button on the wall to let the teller know she was ready to put the empty safe deposit box back.

As she waited, Lizzy tried to wrap her mind about what she now possessed. And figure out what the hell she was going to do with it if Orlando really did have her brother.

* * *

Porter continued scanning the area in front of the bank. No suspicious cars. No men carrying guns. Still, the vise around his chest cinched tighter and tighter each second that Lizzy was out of his sight.

And forget about thinking of her as Elizabeth anymore. Something had changed between them. He couldn't put his finger on what 'it' was, but he'd felt things shift between them last night. That heated kiss before she left the car told him she knew it too.

As his phone buzzed, announcing that he had a new text, he tensed until he saw his brother's brief message. *Lizzy coming outside.*

Only then did that snugness around his chest loosen. Not completely. That wouldn't happen until he saw her with his own eyes.

A few seconds later, tightly clutching the straps to her backpack against her chest, Lizzy walked out of the bank at a brisk pace. She kept her head down but he knew she was aware of everyone around her.

Since the two lane road was deserted, Porter pulled out of the curb side parking spot and flipped a U-turn so he was level with the other curb.

Lizzy didn't pause. She just jumped into the passenger's seat and the moment he saw her face he knew she'd found something. "Drive," was all she said, her tone clipped.

Palm trees and cars flew by at a steady pace as he headed in the general direction of Coconut Grove.

While Lizzy had been inside the bank he'd called Harrison and set it up so that they had a safe house to go to.

Porter still wasn't one hundred percent positive that Orlando didn't have access to their listing of safe houses, but at this point, he and Lizzy needed to get out of Miami proper where Orlando definitely had spies. Keeping an eye on the road and rearview mirror, he began weaving in and out of traffic and making random turns. If they had a tail, he'd know soon enough.

As he drove, Lizzy unzipped the backpack and stuck her hand inside, but didn't pull it back out. A quick glance at her told him all he needed to know. Her lips were pinched tight and her eyebrows drew together in worry.

"You might as well just tell me what you found, Lizzy," he said quietly.

"You've got to promise you'll help my brother." Her voice cracked on the last word.

Damn it. He couldn't tell her no. How did she not realize that by now? Porter bit back a sigh. "Did Benny do something illegal?" *Other than his drug habit.*

"Not exactly, but he's definitely in trouble. In...more ways than one." She bit her bottom lip and clutched the pack closer to her chest with her free hand.

"What's in the backpack?"

"You'll need to read it yourself and we'll want to check some of the entries to make sure all this stuff is legitimate, but it's very damaging to Orlando. There are names of dirty government officials, blackmail information on some of his competitors, lots of nasty stuff. It makes sense why he's after me and why..." She gave him another worried look, "...why he left me a voicemail wanting to trade Benny for this. I don't know for sure but Benny probably told him I had this. Or had access to it or something. Maybe to keep Orlando from killing him or maybe...I don't know." Sighing, she pulled out a thin rectangular notebook.

Porter's hands tightened on the wheel as he looked away from her. "*When* did Orlando call?"

She audibly swallowed. "I got the message before I went in to the bank."

And she hadn't said anything to him. He fought back his temper. "What did he want?"

"His message was cryptic, but it wasn't hard to read between the lines. He thinks I have something he wants—which I do now—and he wants to trade it for Benny. He also inadvertently threatened you. Told me not to say anything to you."

Porter ignored the threat. He didn't give a shit what Orlando said. That man was as good as dead. "Do you know for sure he has your brother?" He glanced at her as they came to a stop light.

Taking her ball cap off, she shook her head. Her dark hair fell around her shoulders in soft, seductive waves.

Something he shouldn't be noticing. "No. Orlando wants me to call him though."

"He'll want to set up a trade as soon as possible." The drug lord wouldn't have made contact with her unless he definitely had Benny. Porter knew Lizzy wouldn't walk away from her brother, but he also knew that whatever was in that notebook was something they couldn't just give back to Orlando. Then the bastard would have no reason to keep her alive. Hell, he'd have even more motivation to kill her now.

"Are you going to tell Grant or Harrison about this?" she asked.

He'd be telling them, but before that he and Lizzy needed to iron out some details. "We'll need to set up a meet with Orlando first."

"You *want* me to call him back?" Shock laced her voice.

He nodded as a plan formed in his mind. With one hand on the wheel, he fished a burner phone out of his back pocket. "Do you need to check your voicemail for Orlando's number?" When she shook her head, he turned the phone on. "Do you trust me?"

She hesitated for a brief moment, then nodded. "Yeah."

"Orlando's going to want to choose the place and the time. You're not going to let him do either. He's got your brother, but you have something he desperately wants. If he kills Benny he'll lose his leverage over you and there will be nothing stopping you from doing whatever you want with the notebook. He's going to want to meet today, but you're going to stall him. Tell him you had to drive a couple hours to get the notebook and that you're going to need to lose me before you meet him. He needs to think you're desperate enough to come alone, but not so desperate that you give him whatever he wants. If you do that, he'll know it's too easy. You can't have a meeting place picked out yet either, but tell him you will the next time you call him back. And you also need to *demand* proof of life for Benny. Now and before we meet him. You got all that?" Porter had been in the protection business for a long damn time. Dealing with hostage situations was rare but Red Stone gave classes to all its security employees. Hell, even law enforcement took classes when they opened them up. This wasn't technically a hostage situation, but it was the same conditions.

And Lizzy was smart. He knew she had practically an eidetic memory so remembering all his instructions wouldn't be difficult. Especially considering it was her brother's life at stake.

CHAPTER ELEVEN

Lizzy took a deep breath and punched in the number she'd committed to memory.

"What?" Orlando's voice grated on her last nerve.

She steeled herself to talk to the monster who had her brother. "I got your message."

"It's taken you a while to call. Your...product might not make it to our trade." He sounded so smug she wanted to jump through the phone line and punch him.

She took a calming breath, trying to keep her emotions out of this. "I want to talk to my brother."

Orlando laughed, which only infuriated her.

Anger was better than fear. "I talk to him or you're not getting *anything*." She put a punch of heat in her voice.

Next to her Porter nodded encouragingly. Seeing his face gave her strength she didn't know she had. Orlando cursed then she heard a soft rustling.

"Lizzy?" Her brother's voice made her throat tighten.

"I'm here. Are you okay? Has he hurt you?"

He laughed though it came out harsh and strained. "I'm fine. Don't give that bastard anything."

"Don't worry about what I'm doing, I just need to know you're okay."

"I'm fine, I promise." His voice sounded a little stronger, but she worried he was lying.

Lizzy looked over at Porter. His knuckles were white as he gripped the steering wheel and his jaw was clenched tight as he watched the road. Having him next to her, supporting her, made even more tears well up. Thankfully they didn't spill over.

"You've heard your brother's voice. Now, we are going to make a trade and you are going to give me exactly what I want. Your brother tells me you have nothing, but he's a sniveling little liar. Or is he? Maybe you have nothing and I should just do away with my problem right now."

Another punch of anger surged through her. Anything was better than fear. She laughed wryly. "Yes, I have what you want. Want me to start reading entries to you?" She flipped the notebook open. "How about I start with one from…five years ago. Looks like Wendell Crane took a payoff from your father in the amount of—"

Orlando cursed so loudly Porter could hear him as she held the phone away from her ear. When Orlando was through with his tirade she put the phone back to her ear. "I'm not meeting you today. I'm too far away.

Benny wasn't stupid, he hid it somewhere you'd never find."

"If you're trying to stall that makes you a very stupid little *puta*, risking your brother's life like that." His voice dripped with venom.

"I would *never* risk my brother's life. I don't give a shit about your stupid book. I just want Benny back." She hoped she'd injected enough fear into her voice to be believable—which the fear wasn't exactly a lie anyway. Before he could speak she continued. "We'll meet early tomorrow morning somewhere of *my* choosing. And you're going to text me a picture of my brother ten minutes before we meet with a newspaper from tomorrow and you will also let me speak to him. And I swear if Benny is injured, you'll *never* see your book. I'll post this on the Internet, mail it out to your competitors, let the whole world know about it."

Porter's eyebrows raised as he pulled up to another stop. For a moment she thought she'd gone too far but he just grinned. She just hoped her demand would keep her brother unharmed.

She snapped her mouth shut as Orlando let out another litany of curses, but eventually the shouts stopped so she said, "I'll call you as soon as I'm in the city." Then she hung up.

Feeling nauseous, she let out a long breath and leaned forward, placing her head between her legs. "I think I'm going to puke," she muttered.

"You were fucking amazing."

Her head snapped in Porter's direction at the surprising curse word. "Really?"

He nodded, something in his pale eyes she couldn't quite define. "Impressive actually."

She felt her cheeks heat up at the unexpected compliment. If she could keep it together long enough to save Benny, everything would be fine.

Now they just had to find a meeting place where they could ambush Orlando. Unfortunately Porter would want to involve Grant and the local police. Something she knew they had to do, but it didn't mean she had to like it.

CHAPTER TWELVE

Lizzy stared at the ceiling, hating this waiting game. Porter was right. She knew that. Waiting to call Orlando was the smart thing to do. She had to play her part if she wanted to keep Benny alive. Rolling on her side she continued blindly staring. This time out the window of the bedroom she was in.

Their security firm had a place in Coconut Grove that was part of their safe houses but rarely used. It was surrounded by trees and other underbrush, not even visible from the cul-de-sac street. In an upper middle class area but very low key, there shouldn't be anyone here who knew Orlando Salas.

Not that anyone had seen either her or Porter to report them in the first place. They'd driven straight into the garage then shut the door before getting out of the vehicle. Now four men Porter said he trusted implicitly were silently patrolling the grounds.

And she and Porter were freaking waiting.

Frustrated, she shoved up from her position and slid off the bed. Porter still hadn't answered all her questions about what their plan was and she needed to talk. He'd told her Grant would be there in a couple hours once he got off work but hadn't said much more than that.

Peeking out in to the hallway, she breathed a sigh of relief to find it empty. Not that she'd really been worried someone was waiting to ambush her, but her nerves were rattled and she figured anything was possible after the last couple days she'd had.

As she went to knock on Porter's door—whose room was right next to hers—she realized it was open a crack. Nudging it with her toe, she called his name. No response. The house seemed eerily quiet, making the tiny hairs on the back of her neck stand on end.

Wrapping her arms around herself she took a cautious step inside. This time she didn't say his name. Fear sank its claws into her chest, sharp and deadly, as she tried to take a calming breath. What if something had happened to Porter?

At a slight squeaking sound she swiveled to find Porter half naked with just a towel around his waist, rivulets of water streaking his very naked chest, and a gun in his hand. "Christ, Lizzy, you scared the shit out of me." He stepped fully out of the bathroom doorway and placed the gun on the five drawer dresser next to it. "Is everything okay?" he asked as he strode to the bed where he'd laid out a pair of jeans and a dark blue polo shirt. He was so...*ripped*. She'd seen him with his shirt off, but now she felt like she was getting a much better show with just a towel hanging from his waist. Her breath caught in her throat.

She didn't care how good he looked.

Yeah right. She almost snorted at herself. The towel around Porter could only cover so much. It was damp and molded to all those muscles, outlining the straining bulge of his thigh muscles and...other stuff.

Something she shouldn't be noticing. Not right now. Not when she wanted to talk to him about something. "When will your brother get here?" she managed to rasp out.

He glanced up at her as he picked up his shirt. "About an hour. Maybe a little longer. Why?" he asked as he turned to fully face her.

She swallowed hard, trying not to watch the way the muscles in his forearms moved as he tossed the shirt over one arm. Her gaze traveled across the broad expanse of his chest, noting more than a handful of scars, including one that webbed out in a sunburst of almost invisible white lines. Against his tan skin the markings were stark against his ribcage. Without thinking, she covered the short distance and placed a hand over the old scar. "What happened here?"

When Porter sucked in a deep breath, her gaze snapped up to meet his. Raw hunger glittered back at her in those pale depths. "Shot. Years ago." His voice was strained.

Instead of pulling away, she lightly rubbed her fingers over the old wound. She hated that he'd ever been in a position to get shot, though she couldn't help but feel incredibly proud of him for all his years in the military.

He made a strangled sound but didn't pull away. Reaching out, he cupped her cheek gently even though she could feel the power practically humming through his fingertips. "You need to leave now or I'll lose all my good intentions." His deep voice rolled through her, waking up the most feminine part of her. Her nipples strained against her top. The man had the ability to turn her into mush without even trying.

She'd come in here only to complain about having to wait to make that call. A call she absolutely couldn't make right now. The next time she called Orlando it would be to set up a meeting place and they didn't have one yet.

Now she just wanted to be with Porter while they had a few precious moments alone. And he was worried about good intentions?

Screw good intentions. She desperately needed to lose herself. To forget about everything going on around them.

Lizzy blindly reached out for his towel and tugged on it. Unable to stop herself, her gaze dipped southward as the piece of cloth fell free.

She swallowed convulsively, unable to tear her gaze away from his hard length. Heat pooled low in her belly, traveling straight to the juncture between her thighs. What she wouldn't give to wrap her hand around him...her mouth around him. She groaned thinking about taking him that way. Seeing the look of pleasure on his face.

"Damn, don't look at me like that." Porter's voice snapped her out of her trance.

As she looked up to meet his gaze, his mouth covered hers, hot and hungry. His fingers threaded through her hair, tightening on her head in a completely dominating grip that made her toes tingle.

She was vaguely aware of the towel falling from her hand, of Porter moving them so that the backs of her knees hit the bed. As her back collided with the soft, fluffy mattress, Porter's rock hard body covered hers.

Still wearing jeans and a T-shirt, she felt overdressed but didn't care as long as she got to touch him. Her hands smoothed over his naked shoulders, down his chest and as she reached between their bodies, he shuddered and pulled back.

"No way," he murmured against her mouth.

Lizzy's eyes flew open as he moved, shimmying down her body. "What are you doing?" After everything they'd been through, she wanted this release with him. Wanted to feel Porter's hands and mouth all over her body. When reality crashed in on her, as she knew it inevitably would, she wanted this memory with Porter. They'd been so damn restrained when they'd been dating and she hadn't been able to get him out of her head since they'd broken up. If she was honest, she didn't want to. She wanted everything he had to offer and only now was she able to fully admit it to herself.

Instead of answering, Porter grasped the button on her jeans. He kept his eyes on her body, watching as he unbuttoned, then unzipped her pants.

Her lower abdomen clenched as he slowly slid them and her skimpy panties down her legs. His heated gaze tracked down her legs until he finally pulled her clothing free and tossed them to the floor. Instantly her thighs fell open a few inches. She wanted to feel his mouth on her so bad she ached for it.

But the request stuck in her throat. They might have been intimate before but they'd never taken things this far.

Slowly, his hands encircled her ankles, holding them in place. His grip wasn't hard but it was enough that she couldn't move.

"Take off your top." A demand, not a request.

The urgency and command in his voice sent a delicious thrill up her spine. Normally she didn't like anyone ordering her around but she would most definitely make an exception for him.

With the late afternoon sun shining through the sheer gold curtains, the room was splashed with orange and gold, creating an erotic atmosphere. Not that she needed anything to set the mood with Porter kneeling in front of her completely naked. His thick erection stood proud against his lower abdomen, telling her exactly how much he wanted her. As he looked at her now with such raw need it was a wonder she'd had any patience at all where Porter was concerned.

Grasping the bottom hem of her shirt, she tugged her top off with shaking hands. Grant might have provided them with clothes, but she still didn't have a bra. As she was bared to Porter for the second time in twenty-four hours, she was overwhelmed by a sudden wave of shyness at being splayed in front of him like this.

"I'm going to taste you." The words seemed to be torn from him and they heated her up from the inside out.

With that statement, any nervousness she might have had disappeared. He wanted her as much as she wanted him.

Lifting her leg, he zeroed in on her inner calf, teasing and raking his teeth over her skin in erotic little nips. Each time his tongue or teeth grazed her skin, she shuddered and the heat between her legs built. Her calf should *not* be an erogenous zone, but the way he made her feel, it was as if she might combust at any moment.

Even though she could have watched him tease her all day, she let her elbows drop as she fell back against the bed. Stretching out, she simply enjoyed the feel of Porter kissing his way up her legs. The higher he moved, the more she instinctively started to tense up, but when he placed firm hands on her inner thighs she forced herself to relax.

With his finger, he gently traced down her wet folds. She slightly jumped at the intimate touch, but when he pushed his finger inside her, she clenched around him. Still, she needed more. She wanted to be completely filled by him.

But he seemed intent on teasing her. Slowly, he drew his finger out then pushed it back in. His rhythm was slow and steady and when he began circling her clit with his tongue, she fisted the sheets beneath her. It was such a torturously unhurried pace, definitely designed to drive her crazy.

Sliding her fingers through his hair, she clutched on to his head. "Faster, Porter," she rasped out.

His chuckle reverberated through her already sensitized body. When he slid another finger inside her she practically shuddered in relief. She wanted more than his fingers but the addition began to ease the ache. As he continued teasing her clit with his tongue, he found a new rhythm.

The closer she was to orgasm, the louder she got. She couldn't help the moans that escaped. The pressure of his tongue and feel of his fingers inside her were too much. Afraid she was gripping his head too tight, she held onto the sheets, clutching them as the first wave of her climax hit.

She'd already been wet and turned on at the sight of Porter half naked so it didn't surprise her how fast he'd pushed her into this release. Her inner walls clenched around him as her back bowed, and she just let the relief pour through her.

When the pressure of his tongue lessened, her eyes flew open. Before she could move, he was on top of her. He still cupped her mound, his fingers fully embedded deep in her as his mouth found hers.

Tasting herself on Porter was wildly erotic. Everything about his kiss was claiming and demanding. As she started to wind her arms around his neck he pulled back.

"Condom," he muttered as he leaned over toward the small nightstand next to the bed.

Apparently this safe house had *everything* they needed. Once he'd grabbed a foil packet, she tried to take it from his hands. She wanted to put it on him, to touch him everywhere.

"Next time," he growled.

The heated note in his voice made her nipples tingle in total feminine appreciation. Porter was always so calm and collected. She loved seeing him lose that edge of control because of her.

And there was no doubt she'd brought this reaction out in him. His sharp cheekbones were flushed, his breathing was harsh and his hands shook as he rolled the condom over his very hard length.

Seeing his hand stroke over himself made her want to do the same, but she knew he wouldn't let her. Porter hated to be out of control and right now he was so close to losing it.

Reaching for him, she grabbed his shoulders and pulled him to her as he repositioned himself in between her legs. He didn't test her slickness but he didn't need to. As he pushed inside her tight sheath she let out a pent up breath she hadn't realized she'd been holding. He filled her completely in a way she hadn't realized she'd needed.

Porter took Lizzy's wrists, guiding them above her head and held them there in an immovable grasp. When she arched her back into him, he savored the feel of her nipples brushing against his chest.

Right now he was on sensory overload. Just looking at her lean, lithe body was enough to make him come. He felt like a randy teenager again. When she'd made a move to put the condom on him, he'd hated telling her no.

The thought of her long elegant fingers wrapped around him...fuck yeah, he wanted that. But not now. Being inside her was better than he'd fantasized about.

And yes, he had imagined. Though nothing could have prepared him for the reality of having sexy-as-hell Lizzy's legs wrapped around his waist as he thrust into her.

Her eyes were heavy lidded, an expression of pure bliss on her face as he held her arms above her head and moved in and out of her body. Only a few inches separated their faces and he couldn't make himself do anything other than watch her reaction.

Knowing he was too close and wanting to watch her come again, he reached between their bodies with his free hand and tweaked the sensitive bundle of nerves he'd enjoyed teasing with his tongue earlier.

At the first stroke of his finger, she jerked underneath him, changing the rhythm of their thrusts.

That's right.

He wanted her to lose control again. Increasing the pressure, he began circling her clit the faster he drove inside her. When she pulled against his grip on her wrists and her back bowed, he knew she was close.

Her inner walls constricted around him, milking him tighter and tighter with each stroke. "Porter," she gasped out and he let her hands go.

Hearing his name on her lips did something primal to him. After this he couldn't walk away from her. If she wanted to keep chasing her brother into shitty situations he'd be right there with her. Walking away simply wasn't an option anymore.

Her fingers dug into his shoulders as another climax tore through her. She moaned out his name again and he covered her mouth with his as his own orgasm hit fast and hard. Holding on to her hips, he knew he'd leave a mark and the most primitive part of him was glad.

Lizzy was his.

As he emptied himself into the condom, her legs tightened around his waist, pulling him tight against her until they both stilled, completely wrapped around one another.

Burying his head in her neck, he inhaled that familiar tropical coconut lime scent he associated with her. It always made him think of being on the beach. "Remind me why we broke up again," he murmured against her soft skin, bracing for her answer and possible rejection.

She let out a long sigh and ran her fingers down his back. She only stopped when she reached his butt. Her fingers dug into his skin. "Because I'm an idiot."

Surprised, he pulled back so he could see her face. Now she placed her palms on his chest and continued before he could say anything. "I pushed you away because of my brother. I...didn't want to admit you were right about him. I love Benny, but..." She swallowed hard and looked away.

No way. He wouldn't let her pull away from him. Not now. Gently he cupped her cheek, drawing her face back toward him.

Her dark eyes glistened with unshed tears. His throat tightened. *Shit.* Why was she crying? Porter tensed, unsure what to do. "What's wrong, honey?"

She swallowed hard again and batted away a tear that strayed down her cheek. "I feel weird telling you all this while you're still inside me."

Porter couldn't help it. A bark of laughter escaped, causing her to chuckle too. When she did, her inner walls tightened around his half-hard cock. Around her he wondered if it would ever go down again. In a few minutes he knew he'd be ready again. Being inside her was only helping that along.

Though he hated doing it, he pulled out of her and disposed of the condom in the nearby wastebasket. Just as quickly he stretched out next to her and pulled her against him so that her head was on his shoulder and her body was half on top of him. Her dark hair pillowed over him. He tightened an arm around her shoulders and stroked down her spine with his other hand. "Why the tears, Lizzy?" he murmured against her hair.

She was silent a moment. "I push away everyone because of Benny. I don't mean to, it just happens."

"Why? You have to know you're only enabling him."

She sniffled once but nodded against his chest, her hair tickling his chin. "When I was fourteen, my uncle tried to rape me."

Porter tensed at her blunt statement, his entire body going still. He didn't comment even though the thought of someone hurting her like that shredded him.

"Benny was sixteen at the time and he stopped him. My uncle had been...abusing Benny for years. Since he was eight. He'd threatened to hurt our parents if Benny told anyone and he was just a scared kid when the abuse began. But when our uncle came after me, Benny lost it and attacked him. Santos and Javier had moved out of the house by then—they were both in college at the time—but they immediately came home ready to spill blood. My parents refused to call the cops though. They wanted to keep it a secret, not wanting to shame our family name. As if me and Benny had done something wrong."

Porter tightened his grip, hating her parents just a little in that moment. "They let your uncle go?"

She let out a shuddering breath. "Yes. He was never allowed in our lives again and they were very protective of both of us after that—buying us whatever we wanted, as if *that* mattered—but they didn't *do* anything. Benny was *distraught*. Our parents finally knew the truth and refused to do anything about it because they were so consumed with our family image. We were so young and had no one else to turn to. By the time I turned eighteen and wanted to tell someone, the police, I don't know...it was too late. Our uncle was dead. Killed in a bar fight. I thought that would give Benny some closure, but it didn't. Drugs don't, gambling doesn't. Nothing seems to fill that void in him."

"Has he tried counseling?" Porter asked quietly, seeing her brother in a different light now.

"A couple times, but he never sticks with it." Her voice broke on the last word and Porter knew he wasn't imagining the wetness on his chest. She wasn't making any overt movements, but he could feel her crying.

"I'm sorry, honey. We're going to get your brother back, I promise." Porter didn't want to push her any further so he just held her. He knew he shouldn't make promises he might not be able to keep, but he'd do whatever it took to get Benny back for Lizzy.

CHAPTER THIRTEEN

Lizzy opened her eyes to a wall of muscle and a spicy scent that was all Porter. She hadn't even realized she'd dozed off. For a brief, terrifying moment she was afraid they'd overslept and she hadn't called Orlando in time, but then she realized the sun was still shining through the sheer curtain.

"You awake?" Porter murmured against the top of her head.

"Mm hmm." She nodded against his chest and shifted closer, savoring the feel of her breasts rubbing against his naked body since she was half-draped over his chest.

His hand strayed down her spine and kept going until he possessively cupped her butt.

"How long was I asleep?" she asked, starting to stir.

"Ten minutes."

She pushed out a relieved breath. They still had time to kill before she had to call Orlando. But first she needed to find out what she was even supposed to say to him. Porter had told her Grant would be coming over to hash out a plan with them. As she started to ask Porter about that, he shifted and reached down until he grabbed her hips.

Moving lightning quick, he moved her until she straddled him. Pushing up on his chest she stared down at him. "What are you doing?" Her hair slid over her chest, covering most of her breasts.

Frowning, he swept her hair to the side and cupped her breasts in a very proprietary manner. "What does it look like?"

Her inner walls clenched as he began to lightly strum her nipples with his thumbs, but when she heard a door shut downstairs she froze.

Porter didn't even pause. He practically tossed her onto the mattress and hurried for his gun. The man didn't even put on clothes as he grabbed it and headed for the bedroom door.

It was probably wrong, but a very small part of her practically drooled watching the way his butt muscles flexed as he moved. The second that thought hit, so did a fresh bolt of terror. Scrambling from the bed she began struggling into her jeans as Porter quietly opened the door.

"Damn it Grant," he muttered and lowered his weapon.

Grant? Crap. Lizzy grabbed her T-shirt and tugged it on. She figured Grant had an idea that something might have been going on between her and Porter but they hadn't actually admitted anything. And she knew Grant would tell Harrison if he saw them in this state together.

Something she didn't even want to think about dealing with right now.

"Hold on—" Porter struggled to keep the door shut, but it popped open and Grant just stood there with a half grin on his face.

"I knew you two were together. Mara denied it but she's very good at evading questions..." He shook his head and his grin grew even bigger. "So, wedding bells in the near future for you two?"

Wedding bells? Oh, God. She and Porter had just slept together for the first time. Thinking about anything else right now just made her head hurt. Feeling incredibly awkward, Lizzy ignored him and looked down to make sure all her clothes were in place. Porter was still freaking naked but he was grabbing for his clothes and cursing under his breath at his brother.

"Get the fuck out of here, Grant. We'll be downstairs in a sec."

"You could say thank you for *this*." He held up two bags. "More clothes for both of you. Mara picked out the stuff for you this time," Grant said to her.

Feeling embarrassed with Porter's state of undress and her no doubt rumpled appearance, Lizzy held her hand out to Grant. "Which one is mine?"

After he handed her one, she mumbled something about freshening up and hurried from the room. She wanted to shower, brush her teeth and God willing, put on a fresh pair of underwear. Hopefully Mara had included some freaking undergarments for her since Grant certainly hadn't included any last time. The thought of him buying her any was weird anyway so it was just as well that he hadn't.

Once alone in the room next to Porter's, she sagged against the back of the door. She wasn't sure exactly what was going on with her and Porter but she knew she didn't want to walk away from him and what had developed between them. She'd opened up to him more than she ever had to anyone. Why had Grant had to bring up anything to do with a wedding? It had probably made Porter uncomfortable. She'd never thought much about marriage before, but the thought of Porter putting a ring on her finger made her cheeks flush and her body grow hot... She groaned. Damn Grant and his big mouth.

Sighing, she shoved a hand through her tangled hair before peering into the bag. There would be time enough to worry about their relationship later. Right now they just needed to focus on getting her brother back.

CHAPTER FOURTEEN

Porter watched Lizzy out of the corner of his eye. They were both sitting in the backseat of an SUV owned by Red Stone Security and heading for the meeting spot with Orlando. The majority of the drive had been in tense silence, not that he blamed her. She just wanted her brother back. He knew that in roughly ten or so minutes, she was going to be very angry with him. But there wasn't anything he could do about it.

Or he wouldn't, even if he could.

Bringing in Grant and the Miami PD was the only option. Once Lizzy had given the notebook to Grant, he'd made a decision and brought his direct boss into the fold. Vice had wanted to bring down Alberto Salas for years, but with him dead, Orlando would be just as good for them. Drugs ran in and out of Miami on a daily basis but most of the big distributors didn't live in the city. They wanted Orlando behind bars.

Orlando's notebook had a lot of damning information on others in the same business. If those individuals found out about Orlando's book someone would definitely come after him. But the info wasn't enough to arrest him for anything because they technically couldn't tie it to him. It wasn't as if he'd put his name and phone number in the front advertising it belonged to him. And it hadn't been obtained legally. With the new information they had on him, they'd be able to shake him up a bit and eventually use the book against him. But no one wanted to wait. Now that Benny was being held hostage the cops had the chance to catch Orlando in the act of committing a crime. Kidnapping was a serious offense.

Unfortunately Lizzy believed that the cops were going to let her go to the meeting place with Orlando. They needed her cooperation because they needed her to call Orlando. So they'd lied to her. And so had Porter.

He hated lying to her of all people, especially after what they'd shared only hours before, but if it meant keeping her safe and saving her brother, he'd make the same decision again.

As they neared the marina where Lizzy was going to tell Orlando to meet her—and where six members of the SWAT team were already set up—the driver slowed and pulled into the parking lot of a deserted international mini mart.

Grant turned around in the front passenger seat. "It's time Lizzy."

Swallowing hard, she looked at Porter with wide eyes. It was two in the morning. Enough time had passed that it was perfect to contact Orlando. The criminal had to believe that Lizzy would never endanger her brother and it wasn't public knowledge that she and Porter had ever dated. If she played it right, she should be able to convince Orlando she'd had to wait to sneak away from Porter's protection.

"You can do this," Porter murmured. He reached out and took her free hand, squeezing reassuringly. While he hated that she was involved in any of this he was proud of her. After the way she'd handled herself on the phone with Orlando yesterday afternoon he had no doubt she could pull this off.

Nodding, she punched in Orlando's number and pressed send. "I want to speak to Benny," she said when someone answered. Moments later her voice softened as she spoke to her brother. Then suddenly she was abruptly cut off and her entire demeanor changed.

Porter knew Orlando had likely taken the phone from Benny. The bastard wouldn't let her talk to her brother very long. Just enough to convince her that he was all right.

Expression hard, she straightened against the seat and she squeezed Porter's hand as she spoke to Orlando. "I'm at the Dinner Key Marina on my parents' boat. Slip 302. It's on the east side—" There was a brief moment of silence. "Well if you know where it is you won't have a problem meeting me there."

Another pause then she said, "It took me a while to lose Porter Caldwell. My boss assigned him to watch me after what happened so it wasn't easy." A brief beat of silence. "I'm not meeting you anywhere else. Benny and I will be leaving on my parents' boat. I'm not letting you try to screw us over."

Porter, Grant and their driver all listened in silence as Lizzy continued convincing Orlando to meet her. When she threatened to hang up and turn the notebook over to his competitors, things wrapped up quickly.

The second she ended the call she dropped the phone into her lap and took a deep breath. Her face was pale and the hand he held was clammy, but when she looked at him all he saw was raw determination in her eyes. "He's going to be there. Let's go."

Porter shot Grant a quick look. His brother's face was grim but he didn't say anything, just slid out of the passenger seat. The moment he'd shut the door behind him, the vehicle jerked to life as the driver steered out of the parking lot.

Lizzy looked out the tinted window as Grant got into another SUV then she turned back to Porter, confusion on her face. "What's going on?"

"He's heading to the marina to get in place with the rest of the guys." Grant and his boss had only involved a very small fraction of the SWAT team and a few guys from vice they trusted. There was no way in hell they'd chance this leaking to Orlando. Not when he was finally within reach.

She withdrew her hand from his. "Why aren't we going with him?"

Porter wanted to reach for her again, but decided against it. "Honey, they can't allow a civilian to be part of this operation."

A frown marred her lips and he could see the understanding in her eyes. "So...you lied to me?"

"I didn't—"

"Yes, you did. You sure as hell didn't correct Grant when he told me I'd be waiting on that boat to lure Orlando. When he reassured me his team would be covering me the entire time and that they only needed to bring Orlando out into the open to prove he'd kidnapped Benny. You sat there and held my hand and didn't say one damn word!" She crossed her arms over her chest and scooted a little closer to the door—away from him.

"I promised you I'd help bring Benny home alive. If you refused to work with them and didn't call Orlando, or tried to meet him on your own, you and Benny would have been killed."

"Why didn't you just tell me the truth and give me a chance to make the right decision?" she asked quietly.

The accusations he saw in her dark eyes sliced right through his chest, making him feel even shittier. "They needed to make sure you would call Orlando. This operation had to go off without a hitch. Everything you said to him needed to be believable."

"Did you know about this before or after we..." Even in the darkened vehicle he could see her cheeks flush red. She glanced at the driver then back at Porter.

"After, but...I knew that once they had the notebook you wouldn't like whatever plan they came up with." Might as well go with full honesty.

Her lips thinned. "I don't understand why I can't be there. Grant said Orlando was never going to make it to the boat. What if he gets to the marina and doesn't have Benny? What if—"

"You're a civilian. There is no way in hell they'd allow you to even remotely be a part of this. There's an undercover policewoman on the boat so in case he sends someone to scout it out first, 'you' will be there. But you have no place there." Something he had no doubt she understood perfectly well.

With her arms crossed, she turned in her seat away from him and stared out the window. "You shouldn't have lied to me."

He scrubbed a hand over his face. "I...I know. And I'm sorry for that. But not for anything else. Even if for some insane reason Grant would have allowed you to be involved, I wouldn't have."

Her head whipped back around, her eyes blazing. "You wouldn't have *allowed* me?"

"Damn straight." If she thought he'd ever let her walk head first into danger, she was out of her mind.

Her dark eyes narrowed and she opened her mouth, no doubt to blast him, when his cell phone buzzed. Porter tensed when he saw Grant's name. "Yeah?"

"Lizzy still with you?" His voice was grim.

Of course she was. Porter tightened his grip on the phone. "What's going on?"

"I need to talk to her."

"Grant—"

"Sorry man, I've gotta talk to Lizzy." There was no room for argument in his brother's voice.

That alone told Porter something very bad had happened. *Please don't let it be Benny*, he silently prayed. His gut twisted as he handed the phone to her. "It's Grant, he wants to talk to you."

Her eyebrows drew together. "What about?" Porter shook his head as she took the phone and held it up to her ear. "Grant?...Wha...I don't understand...But...How..." Tears started rolling down her cheeks as she dropped the cell.

Porter picked it up and started to speak to his brother when Lizzy broke into a sob. "Benny's dead."

A vise tightened around Porter's chest. *Shit*. He ended the call and shoved the phone in his pocket. He'd get the details later. Right now Lizzy needed comforting. He attempted to pull her into his arms but she jerked away from him, slapping at his chest. "Don't touch me!"

He reached for her again, desperately wanting to offer support. "Lizzy—"

With a pale face and shaking hands, she shoved his hands away. "Oh God, I'm going to be sick." She slapped a hand over her mouth. Tears tracked down her cheeks as she struggled with her seatbelt so he unsnapped it.

Her face was ashen and she made a blind grab for the door handle so he tapped their driver and motioned to the gas station they were approaching on the right side of the road. A neon sign proclaimed they were open twenty-four hours.

Nodding, the guy pulled in to the brightly lit station. There weren't any other cars there so they got a spot right out front. Lizzy—still holding a hand over her mouth—jumped from the vehicle and darted for the glass doors before Porter had even unbuckled himself.

He thought about calling Grant but decided to go in and wait for her. She'd likely want some privacy while she got sick but he'd be waiting outside the door when she was done.

The store was quiet, the young female Asian clerk texting on her phone barely glanced his way when he entered. Once outside the unisex bathroom door, he knocked lightly. "Lizzy?"

"Go away." Her voice was muffled but he could hear the tears in it.

"Lizzy—"

"Just give me a couple minutes!" She sounded angry, not that he blamed her. He knew once it fully hit her that Benny was dead she'd be a wreck. And he planned to be there for her.

He wanted to call Grant back and demand answers. Wanted to know how the hell Benny had been killed and who had done it. Guilt ran rampant through Porter as he wondered if they should have done something differently. He'd never know until he knew the details.

When he heard Lizzy quietly crying inside the restroom it was like knives being dragged across his skin. He raised his hand to knock again but knew her well enough that she wouldn't appreciate the intrusion. Hating that she was stuck in a fucking gas station bathroom crying, he took a step back and headed down the aisles until he reached a cooler of doors and pulled out a water bottle for her. He might not be able to ease any of her sorrow but he could at least take care of her the best way he knew how.

When he heard the bell above the door jingle he automatically glanced toward the front of the store. A young Spanish guy, maybe in his early twenties, was at the counter buying cigarettes. That wasn't what interested Porter though. The guy had a black and blue bandana shoved in his back pocket.

Ducking down, Porter made his way over a few more aisles until he had a perfect view of the front of the station. There was a blue muscle car that looked just like the one he'd seen outside the motel. There was no one else inside though. So this guy was alone.

Porter peered around the edge of the aisle to get a good look at the guy. Just flirting with the sales clerk, not paying any attention to his surroundings. Which meant he hadn't been following them. The area of town they were in wasn't exactly a rough neighborhood but it was on the cusp of a bad neighborhood. The same one the Seventy Ninth Street gang frequented.

Just great.

Any other day it wouldn't have mattered. Setting the water on the ground, Porter hurried around the corner of the aisle so that he was walking parallel to the glass windows. He wanted to get as close to the door as possible, but still remain hidden from the guy.

Porter was too far away to get to Lizzy and there was a big gap of space between the aisles of food and the short hallway where the restroom was. Nowhere for him to hide his approach. He just prayed she stayed inside. If she did, they wouldn't have any issues. If she came out and the guy at the register recognized her, things could get shitty.

As the guy pocketed his change then grabbed cigarettes and a candy bar, Porter saw Lizzy stride out of the restroom. Her head was down as she wiped tears from her cheeks and her skin was abnormally pale beneath the harsh fluorescent lights.

The young male hadn't noticed her. His back was to Lizzy as he turned toward the front doors. Crouching a few inches lower, Porter remained hidden behind the first row of canned sodas and beers. Every muscle in his body was tense as he readied himself for a fight even while he prayed it wouldn't come to that.

For a brief moment, he let a small breath of relief escape. Then the guy turned back around.

It was as if everything moved into slow motion. The gang member headed back for the register but paused when he saw Lizzy. He reached into his pocket and Porter took a step forward, only stopping when the guy pulled a phone out.

He looked at the screen, then back at Lizzy. *Then* he reached into his jacket pocket.

Porter didn't pause to wait and see if he pulled out a weapon. Silently, he moved out from behind the long row and rushed at the guy.

Though he didn't make a sound, the clerk made a slight yelping sound, causing the dark-haired guy to turn in Porter's direction. In the guy's hand was a .45 semi-automatic pistol.

Porter was vaguely aware of the woman behind the register screaming and Lizzy letting out a strangled sound, but all his focus was on the gang member. Without losing momentum, he opened his arms and tackled him, not giving him a chance to raise his weapon. Porter had one of his own, but this wasn't a situation that called for it.

As he made contact, the guy let out a loud grunt as he slammed into the tile. His head hit the floor and bounced up. Porter heard the gun clatter to the floor, but that wasn't enough. With a sharp punch, he jabbed the guy in the ribs. This guy had tried to kill Lizzy, or scare the hell out of her, twice.

The dark haired guy began to struggle and even though Porter would have loved to beat the shit out of him, he wrenched one arm up and twisted him over until he was face down. When he tried to fight Porter, he raised the arm higher so that if the guy moved, his arm would snap. A dark part of Porter wouldn't mind if the guy's arm broke. It wouldn't be punishment enough.

Out of the corner of Porter's eye he watched Lizzy picking up the fallen gun. A quick glance at her made his gut clench. She looked almost frozen with shock. Her eyes were wide and her face even paler than before. "Are you okay, Porter?" Her voice was wobbly and watery and damn it, he wanted to slam this guy's head into the tile again for that.

"I'm fine, honey. Get behind that aisle and keep the gun close to you." He nodded with his head, hoping she'd follow directions. Once she was out of sight, he glanced over his shoulder at the door. He twisted the gang member's body so that they were facing the front of the store and Porter's back wasn't exposed.

Porter looked at the sales clerk who was just gaping at them. "Call the police."

His words seemed to snap her out of her trance. Nodding, she scrambled with her cell phone and dialed.

Porter was about to tell Lizzy to get their driver when he spotted the guy rushing toward the front door. "I called the cops when I saw what was going on. I'll stand watch by the door," he said quietly as soon as he was inside.

Porter nodded silent thanks. In case this shithead's friends were around, he needed someone to watch his back. Underneath him the guy was muttering curses about how this was a big mistake but Porter ignored him.

Porter would have liked to tell their driver to put Lizzy in the SUV but he didn't want her outside and out of his sight. He needed her close.

All Porter cared about was getting Lizzy back to his place. While he wanted to know what the hell had gone wrong with the sting operation to bring down Orlando, it was on the backburner of his mind right now. Lizzy was obviously in shock from her brother's death and he needed to get her to safety before the numbness faded and the true grief set in. Unfortunately he knew that they'd be stuck dealing with questions and would have to make statements. When he risked a glance in her direction, he wished he hadn't. She was peering around the aisle he'd told her to duck behind, staring at the gang member on the floor.

Dried tears marked down her face, leaving trails of mascara smudged under her eyes. Her face was pale and her dark eyes full of sorrow.

What Porter wouldn't give to gather her into his arms and just hold her. He inwardly cursed as he pinned the gang member to the floor. Somehow he was going to help Lizzy get through this.

It felt like an eternity passed, but minutes later blue and red flashing lights filled the parking lot. Almost immediately a stocky patrolman took the gang member into custody. The punk cursed at the cop telling him this was all a big misunderstanding as he was being dragged from the store. Considering there were three witnesses and if the video surveillance worked, further proof of what he'd been about to do, Porter wasn't concerned about the guy. The gang member would be going to jail for a long time.

But that was the least of his worries right now. Men and women in uniform milled in and out of the store and even though Lizzy shrugged Porter's arm off when he tried to embrace her, she stayed near him, watching everything unfold around them.

After answering a couple dozen questions over and over, the cops finally let them go without taking them down to the station for questioning. Porter knew the only reason they were being let go was because of his brother Grant and because Porter worked for Red Stone Security. They hired a lot of off duty cops for local security work and had a good working relationship with the department.

Once they were let go, he settled Lizzy into the back seat and slid in next to her. "It's too soon to go back to your place, Lizzy. Not until we know if Orlando has called off his dogs. Considering what happened at the gas station…Ah, do you want to go to my home or a hotel or a safe house?" He'd take her any damn place she pleased as long as it wasn't her home. That was just too dangerous.

"Take me to my parents." Her voice was monotone as she stared out the window at the patrol cars and police officers.

"Honey—"

"Don't call me honey! Don't…just don't. I want to go to my parents' house." Her voice broke on the last word, absolutely shredding him.

Porter glanced at the driver and gave him the address. Once they steered out of the parking lot, he turned back to her. She still only gave him her profile, refusing to glance in his direction. "I'm so sorry about Benny."

She whipped around to look at him, tears in her eyes. "Don't say his name. I don't want to talk about him with you. I just want to..." Now the tears started falling. Turning in her seat, she gave him her back. Her fragile shoulders shook with each silent sob, breaking his heart.

He started to place a comforting hand on her back, but stopped himself at the last moment. She'd made it clear she didn't want his help. Feeling more helpless than he ever had—including when he'd been in the Marines and had been left behind enemy lines for two months without a way to contact his team—he sat there staring at her, unable to do a damn thing.

When they made it to her parents' house, she got out of the vehicle without a backward glance at him. While he wanted to chase after her he knew it would be a fruitless effort. He couldn't force her to let him comfort her. To take care of her. If he tried she'd just push him further away than she already had.

Feeling numb, he instructed the driver to take him down to the station. He knew that's where Grant would be and he planned to get answers about what had gone wrong tonight and why Lizzy's brother was dead.

CHAPTER FIFTEEN

One week later

Lizzy shut the front door of her house and sagged against it. After Benny's funeral, then the gathering at her parents' house afterward, she just wanted to sink to the floor and sleep for days. There had been too many people there. Most of whom hadn't even known her brother or cared about him. But they'd come because her parents were wealthy and well known in Miami.

She'd been staying at her parents' house since then. Porter had continued to call her and she'd talked to him a few times, but she couldn't bear to see him. Or to be alone with him. He made her happy and was so damn understanding about everything and she didn't want that right now. She didn't have a right to be in love and happy when Benny was dead.

At least Orlando was in prison, as were the gang members who had targeted her on his behalf. The cops didn't think they'd be a threat to her anymore because she wasn't going to have to testify against them. They'd turned on Salas and had cut a deal so her testimony wasn't necessary. Part of that deal had meant admitting guilt to coming after her. It was the only way the state's attorney would even consider a deal for less jail time. Considering they had one of the guys on video at that gas station drawing his weapon on her, taking a deal had been the smart move.

And Orlando had a hell of a lot more problems than her at the moment. She wasn't even a blip on his radar now that news of his little black book had gotten out. Apparently many of his competitors were feeling very homicidal over it. If he was lucky he'd survive his imprisonment and stay in as long as he could, because if he got out, he wouldn't last long on the outside. Though something told her that he wouldn't be untouchable in jail. If someone wanted him dead bad enough, it would happen.

And if something happened to him she sure wouldn't lose any sleep over it. Especially since she had some homicidal thoughts herself considering Benny had been killed because of him. She still hadn't received a straight answer on who shot her brother, but he'd been gunned down in the crossfire between Orlando and the Miami PD at the marina. One of Orlando's men had apparently seen one of the SWAT members and things had gone crazy in seconds.

As she pushed away from her slumped position at the door, the bell rang and she nearly jumped out of her skin. Peering through the peephole, she saw two men in black suits and someone in between them. He was wearing a hoodie and...Lizzy's heart stopped for a moment. She jerked the door open, trying to catch her breath.

Before she could move or speak, the two men in suits barreled past her, dragging her with them until they shut the door. But she didn't even mind being manhandled. Not when she was staring at Benny.

Unless he was a ghost and she'd officially lost her mind...Reaching out, she shoved the hoodie back and touched his face.

Benny's smile was tentative as he stepped forward. "I'm so sorry, sis," he whispered.

Unable to stop herself, she threw her arms around Benny's neck and squeezed hard. Her throat was too tight to speak and if this was all a dream, she didn't want to wake up. When she eventually tried to talk, nothing came out except for tears which streamed down her cheeks.

She wasn't sure how much time passed, but eventually Benny took her arms and entangled himself from her. "I don't have much time—"

"We need to talk and you need to listen, ma'am," one of the men in suits who she'd forgotten was even there, said softly.

Wiping at the tears that just wouldn't seem to stop, she turned and nodded. "Okay," she said in a raspy voice. Grabbing Benny's hand, she motioned to the living room and pulled him with her. She refused to let go of his hand. Was afraid that if she did, he'd disappear.

The two men entered first and one of them drew her blinds shut. With wobbly legs, she made her way to the long couch and sat, pulling her brother with her. "I thought you were dead. I went to your funeral." Her voice cracked and she had to swallow hard before continuing. "Does anyone else know about this? Do Javier and Santos? They were heartbroken at your—"

Clearing his throat, the tall, dark haired man with flawless ebony skin sat at the loveseat across the coffee table from them. "Ma'am, your brother has been placed in WITSEC."

"The Witness Security Program?" She blinked, looking from Benny to who she assumed must be a US Marshall.

"You've heard of us?"

Snorting, she nodded. "I watch television." There was a new show about the WITSEC program she was addicted to. She wasn't sure how much of it was real and how much was bogus, but she'd at least heard of them.

"Your brother is in the program and one of his only stipulations..." The man sighed, as if it pained him to speak, "...was that you know he wasn't dead. He said he wouldn't join otherwise. Now, you get two minutes alone, but we're still listening so Benny, you don't tell her where you'll be living or what your new name is."

The man stood, nodding at the other man hovering by the window and they both exited into her foyer, leaving Lizzy alone with Benny.

Two minutes. Lizzy felt as if her heart would jump right out of her chest. Her brother was still alive! "Why are you going into the program? Why did you fake your own death?"

Benny scrubbed a hand over his face. A face that looked surprisingly fresh and full of hope. He didn't have that gray pallor she'd come to associate with his drug problems. "That wasn't my idea. Eventually it'll come out that I'm still alive but for now they want everyone to think I'm dead. The state's attorney is building a case against Orlando and his entire organization so until a trial date is set, I'll be in protection. In case anything else falls through, I'm going to be a star witness. He kidnapped and attempted to kill me. That alone would be enough to put me in the program, but he likes to talk and...well, he's got a big mouth and he assumed I'd be dead soon so he didn't mind talking business in front of me. Arrogant bastard," he muttered, shaking his head.

"So how long will you be gone?" she asked, unable to hide the hope in her voice that it wouldn't be very long.

He shook his head as he threaded his fingers through hers, holding her hands tight. "I have no idea, but don't get your hopes up. This might be a permanent thing."

As her throat tightened and she felt tears start to well up, he shook his head and pulled her into a tight hug. "I love you more than anyone, *hermanita*. For the first time in my life I feel like I can give something back. Make a difference. I can't tell you where I'm going or anything about my new life, but they've already lined up a counseling program for me to get a handle on all my addictions. Knowing you showed up at Orlando's house because of me..." He shook his head. "If I could go back in time I'd redo a lot of things, but dragging you down with me was a shitty thing to do. And I'm not just talking about this mess with Orlando. You're the best sister anyone could have ever asked for. I don't know why you stuck with me so long, but...I'm sorry for all the grief I caused you and the danger I put you in." His voice shook as he pulled back from the embrace.

She squeezed his hands in her own. "Benny, you don't have to apologize."

He grunted. "Yeah, I do. I got a raw deal with our parents. Hell, we both did. But I'm taking control of my life and it feels good. You're the only person who ever believed in me, who ever...really loved me, I think. I love you so much and I know how much you've sacrificed over the years looking out for me. Please know that I understand and appreciate all you've done. More than you'll ever know. I'm going to miss you, but I'm glad I'm getting a fresh start."

"I'm going to miss you so much." She could barely squeeze the words out.

Benny drew her into another tight embrace. She savored the feel of her brother's arms around her, knowing it would be the last hug they shared for a very long time.

As they pulled back, he paused for a moment, as if trying to decide what to say. Finally he spoke. "The Caldwell brothers know about me going into the program."

"*What?*" If she hadn't been sitting, she was sure her knees would have given out.

Benny nodded. "I just thought you should know. Grant is part of the select few who know I didn't die last weekend and...as of yesterday, Porter and Harrison know too. They've both got classified clearances, but I think the real reason they know is because of Grant's insistence. He told me that you and Porter, uh, well...anyway, your boyfriend knows too."

"He's not my boyfriend." The words were automatic. Hell, she didn't know what she and Porter were now.

Benny snorted softly and stood, pulling her up with him. "I've got to go. Just know that I love you and I'm finally...content. If they let me I'll write letters to you, but I don't think that's a possibility. You can't tell anyone else about this, not even our parents."

She'd been keeping secrets from the time she was fourteen. Keeping this from her parents wouldn't be a problem. Especially considering the way they'd failed to help her brother or her when they'd needed it most. She nodded and gave Benny one more hug. Then, he was gone. Out of her house as if he'd never been there. After watching her brother leave in an SUV with tinted windows, she shut her front door with shaking hands, unsure how to feel.

She was thrilled her brother wasn't dead, but couldn't believe he was being placed in the WITSEC program. Or that Porter knew her brother was alive. Benny said he'd only found out yesterday and she'd been ignoring his calls the past few days. She thought she'd seen him at the funeral today, but couldn't be sure. There had been so many people.

She'd been there only long enough to be polite, then slipped out. Sighing, she toed off her shoes and unzipped her simple black dress as she headed for her bedroom. She didn't bother hanging it up, just let it pool in a messy lump near the foot of her bed before climbing under the covers.

Her eyes felt heavy and gritty. The past week she'd barely slept. She'd cried more than she'd imagined possible and now it finally felt as if an entire week of needed sleep was crashing in on her. Even though it was daylight, she was unable to stay awake any longer. Pulling the covers up to her neck, she let the blessed peacefulness of sleep overtake her.

* * *

Porter's heart beat erratically as he eased open the backdoor to Lizzy's house. Her place was eerily silent, but her car was outside. He'd rung her doorbell and called her cell, but she hadn't responded. He'd wanted to talk to her at the funeral earlier, but she'd been surrounded by her family and hell, she hadn't been returning his calls. Confronting her at Benny's funeral would have been a mistake.

But he couldn't take it anymore. He wouldn't let her erect these walls between them. Not after what they'd been through together. More than anything he was worried about her. Especially when he'd heard the faint jingle of her cell phone inside a few minutes ago. The house was just too damn quiet for her to be in there and simply ignoring him.

Withdrawing his SIG, he crept silently through her dark kitchen. A single light above the sink area was the only source of light. As he continued sweeping the house, his alarm grew. Once he'd cleared the living room and guest bathroom, he headed down her hallway.

He froze when he heard a squeaking sound coming from her bedroom. Increasing his pace he hurried down the rest of the hallway and stopped only when he reached the partially open door.

Easing it open with his foot, he took a step inside. For a moment, time seemed to stand still. Lizzy stood near her bathroom door wearing a bra and panties and carrying a glass of water. When she saw him she let out an ear piercing scream.

He immediately tucked his weapon into the back of his pants and held up his hands. "It's just me!"

Lizzy's hand flew to her chest and she slammed the glass down on the antique desk next to the door. "What the hell are you doing here? Are you trying to scare me to death?"

"I'm sorry. I called and rang the doorbell and..." Now he felt like a fucking stalker. After everything she'd been through he'd just been worried. Not that she'd be suicidal or anything, but shit, he'd been concerned. "I'm sorry, Lizzy."

She dropped her hand and took a tentative step forward. The light from the bathroom shone around her, illuminating her long, lithe frame. "How'd you get in?"

"I was worried about you so, I, uh, picked the lock to your backdoor." He swallowed hard, fighting back the guilt inside him.

Instead of reaming him out, she just stared at him for a long moment. "Benny came by today."

She knew. *Thank God.* "I just found out last night from Grant. I tried calling, but..." She hadn't answered, something they both already knew. "How are you?" It'd been hell to watch her grieve at the funeral and not be able to tell her Benny was alive.

Shaking her head, she walked to the end of her bed and sank down on the edge of the mattress. "I have no idea. I..." Her voice cracked and she wrapped her arms around herself in a protective gesture.

Screw it. He crossed the distance between them and gathered her in his arms. To his relief, she didn't pull away. She molded to him, wrapping her arms around his neck and plastering herself against his body.

"I'm sorry I've been so distant this week. I didn't know how to talk to you," she whispered against his neck.

The feel of her hot breath sent a shiver through him. Wanting to feel all of her against him, he picked her up and stretched her out on the bed. After quickly divesting his weapon on the nightstand and taking off his shoes, he slid in next to her and held her tight.

"I'm not walking away from you, Lizzy. I'm glad your brother is alive but even if he'd died, this thing between us...I don't want anyone else and I'm tired of fighting it. You're stubborn and sexy and you're it for me," he murmured against the top of her head.

He felt her smile against his chest. "Oh, really?"

"Yeah, really."

Her smile grew wider. "Good. I know I've been a jerk the last week, but...I just didn't know how to deal with anything. I felt guilty that I was alive and Benny wasn't, like it was somehow my fault. That maybe if I'd been at the marina things would have ended differently. I was hurting and knew I'd take all my anger out on you. I didn't want to bring you down with me."

"I want for better or worse from you, Lizzy. You can bring me down all you want." He slid a hand down her back, snagging the back of her bra as he moved south.

She shuddered against him, arching her back into his chest as she lifted her head. With the dim light from the bathroom illuminating the room, it was hard to see much, but her eyes were filled with heat. "For better or worse, huh?" she whispered, her voice unsure.

He nodded. "This week without you has been hell. I love you, Lizzy and I won't let you walk away from me."

"*Won't?*" She lifted a dark eyebrow as she shifted her body so that she fully straddled him. Looking down at him, she reached behind her back and unhooked her bra.

As it slid down her arms, displaying her breasts, his brain short circuited for a moment. Eventually he found his voice. "You're mine," he growled, unable to keep the hunger out of his voice.

She leaned down until their noses almost touched. "I love you too, Porter."

His mouth was on hers before she could say another word. In a few quick moves he had her pinned beneath him as he took her mouth in a frenzied kiss. Heat built inside him like a raging inferno as she grappled with his shirt and he struggled to get his pants off.

After being deprived of her sweet body for a week he knew this first time between them would be fast and hard. But he'd take it slow the second time around. And there would definitely be a second time tonight. Maybe a third.

Lizzy had gotten under his skin in the best way and just the thought of being inside her again was making him a little bit crazy. Even when he knew this was the first night of many. Because he'd been serious about for better or worse.

He wanted the whole package from her. Marriage, a house, kids, everything. The woman was absolute grace under fire and her loyalty to her brother was simply amazing. He knew she'd make a perfect life partner. And that's what he wanted. Lizzy as his partner for life— through the good and the bad times.

Thank you for reading No One to Trust. I really hope you enjoyed it and that you'll consider leaving a review at one of your favorite online retailers. If you don't want to miss any future releases, please feel free to join my newsletter. I only send out a newsletter for new releases or sales news. Find the signup link on my website: http://www.katiereus.com

COMPLETE BOOKLIST

Red Stone Security Series
No One to Trust
Danger Next Door
Fatal Deception
Miami, Mistletoe & Murder
His to Protect
Breaking Her Rules
Protecting His Witness
Sinful Seduction
Under His Protection
Deadly Fallout
Sworn to Protect

The Serafina: Sin City Series
First Surrender
Sensual Surrender
Sweetest Surrender
Dangerous Surrender

Deadly Ops Series
Targeted
Bound to Danger
Chasing Danger (novella)
Shattered Duty
Edge of Danger
A Covert Affair

Non-series Romantic Suspense

Running From the Past
Dangerous Secrets
Killer Secrets
Deadly Obsession
Danger in Paradise
His Secret Past
Retribution

Paranormal Romance
Destined Mate
Protector's Mate
A Jaguar's Kiss
Tempting the Jaguar
Enemy Mine
Heart of the Jaguar

Moon Shifter Series
Alpha Instinct
Lover's Instinct (novella)
Primal Possession
Mating Instinct
His Untamed Desire (novella)
Avenger's Heat
Hunter Reborn
Protective Instinct (novella)

Darkness Series
Darkness Awakened
Taste of Darkness
Beyond the Darkness
Hunted by Darkness

Into the Darkness

ABOUT THE AUTHOR

Katie Reus is the *New York Times* and *USA Today* bestselling author of the Red Stone Security series, the Moon Shifter series and the Deadly Ops series. She fell in love with romance at a young age thanks to books she pilfered from her mom's stash. Years later she loves reading romance almost as much as she loves writing it.

However, she didn't always know she wanted to be a writer. After changing majors many times, she finally graduated summa cum laude with a degree in psychology. Not long after that she discovered a new love. Writing. She now spends her days writing dark paranormal romance and sexy romantic suspense. For more information on Katie please visit her website: www.katiereus.com. Also find her on twitter @katiereus or visit her on facebook at: www.facebook.com/katiereusauthor.

Printed in Great Britain
by Amazon